"Follow that bus!"

"Are you sure they're not still here somewhere?" I asked Stephanie. We had looked all over the street for Patti and Lauren, but it was pretty obvious they were gone.

"Kate, we've looked everywhere but under the manholes," Stephanie said with a sigh. "They're on that bus!"

I snapped my fingers. "I know what we should do! Let's take a cab after the bus."

"That won't work," Stephanie replied.

"Sure it will! People do it in the movies all the time. We just get in a cab and say, 'Follow that bus!' "

"It might have worked if we'd done it five minutes ago," said Stephanie. "But that bus is long gone!"

Look for these and other books
in the Sleepover Friends Series:

Patti's City Adventure

Susan Saunders

AN
APPLE
PAPERBACK

SCHOLASTIC INC.
New York Toronto London Auckland Sydney

ISBN 0-590-44356-9

Copyright © 1991 by Daniel Weiss Associates, Inc. All rights reserved. Published by Scholastic Inc. APPLE PAPERBACKS is a registered trademark of Scholastic Inc. SLEEPOVER FRIENDS is a registered trademark of Daniel Weiss Associates, Inc.

12 11 10 9 8 7 6 5 4 3 2 1   1 2 3 4 5 6/9

Printed in the U.S.A.   28

First Scholastic printing, August 1991

Patti's City Adventure

Chapter
1

"I can't believe we're finally getting to the city again," Stephanie Green said, rolling down her car window. "This is going to be great! I can't wait to go shopping at Leland's, and Mixed Mode, and — "

"Hold it," I said. "We're not going to spend the whole forty-eight hours shopping." Stephanie gets carried away at the *thought* of new stores to buy clothes in — if you're not careful, you end up trailing after her to every store in town. Not that we have too many great clothing stores in Riverhurst, but you know what I mean.

Oh, by the way — I'm Kate Beekman. Stephanie is one of my best friends, along with Patti Jenkins and Lauren Hunter. The four of us were going to spend the weekend in the city to celebrate Patti's eleventh birthday. Since Patti's parents wanted to spend Patti's birthday with her, too, they were driving us down, and we were all going to stay with friends of theirs. Patti's little brother, Horace, was also in the minivan with us. He was sitting up front with Mr. and Mrs. Jenkins.

Patti and Stephanie both used to live in the city. For me and Lauren, though, going there was a big deal. There was a lot I wanted to see and do over the weekend.

Lauren sighed and stared out the window of the Jenkins's minivan. "This trip is longer than I remembered," she grumbled.

"We're almost there," Patti told her. "It's about a half hour more."

"A half hour!" Lauren groaned. Needless to say, she isn't fond of long car trips. We had already been driving for two hours. It was Friday night — we'd left right after school.

I had a feeling I knew why Lauren was so miserable. "Would this make you feel any better?" I asked. I reached into my overnight bag and pulled out a plastic container.

"What's that?" asked Stephanie.

"Something to tide us over until dinner," I said.

2

I opened the container and pulled out a huge bunch of grapes.

"All right!" Lauren cried.

Patti's mother turned around in her seat. "Everything okay back there?"

"Everything's fine," Patti replied. She ripped off a smaller bunch and passed them to her mom. "Kate brought a snack."

Lauren rested her head on the back of the seat and dropped a grape into her mouth. "Yum."

It doesn't take much to make Lauren happy. She loves to eat. She can eat whatever she wants, and stay as skinny as a rail. I call her the Bottomless Pit.

If Lauren's favorite thing is food, then mine is movies. I love to watch them, and I do whenever I get the chance. In fact, I was kind of upset that we were going to miss "Friday Night Chillers" on Channel 21 that night — it was a tradition with me. With all four of us, actually, since we spend almost every Friday night together.

Way back in kindergarten, Lauren and I had started the tradition of Friday-night sleepovers, and we've been doing it ever since. When Stephanie moved to Riverhurst, two years ago, she became part of them (even though the two of us did *not* get along at first. Now we're friends, though. We still disagree about things sometimes, but it's usually not very serious.) Then Patti came to town this year, and joined in, too.

"Do you think we'll be able to have a regular sleepover at the Mitchells'?" Lauren asked, almost as if she were reading my mind. I guess that's what happens when you've been friends with someone as long as Lauren and I have been friends.

"I don't see why not," said Patti. "I think we're crashing in the living room."

"Once everyone goes to bed, the place will be all ours," said Stephanie. "And," she added, tapping Lauren on the shoulder, "we'll have easy access to the kitchen."

Horace turned around and grinned at us. "Hey, Patti, can we play a game?" He's only seven years old, but he's a real brain. I could just see him wanting to play magnetic chess or something.

"Okay," Patti said. "What should we play?"

"How about Truth or Dare?" asked Stephanie.

Patti hit her playfully on the arm. "Come on, this isn't a sleepover," she said.

"What's Truth or Dare?" asked Horace.

"Never mind," Patti told him. "I'll tell you later. How about a game of Hangman?"

4

"Yeah!" Horace agreed. Patti got out her notebook and leaned forward in her seat so she and Horace could play.

Stephanie and I leaned forward so we could talk to Lauren. "Do you think she has any idea what we have planned?" whispered Stephanie.

Lauren shook her head. "She thinks we're just having a party at the Mitchells' tomorrow night."

"I can't wait to see the look on her face when we go to that restaurant," I said softly. The three of us planned to take Patti to this new, really cool restaurant we had seen in our favorite magazine, *Teen Topics*. Supposedly it was *the* place for kids our age (okay, maybe a little older) to hang out. Stars showed up there all the time, too. We'd called ahead and made a reservation and arranged to have a cake brought out, and the whole staff was going to sing "Happy Birthday." I couldn't wait to see the look on Patti's face! She's really shy, so I knew she'd be embarrassed, but I also knew she'd be totally excited.

Half an hour later, we could see the city skyline in the distance. It was really pretty. The sun was just setting, and some of the skyscrapers had neat lights and shapes at the top. I wondered what it would be like to live there all the time.

The Mitchells lived about twenty miles outside

the city. We pulled up in front of their house at about six o'clock. "Finally!" Lauren cried, jumping out of the van. She stretched her arms over her head.

The front door of the house opened, and a boy who looked like he was about thirteen walked out onto the front steps.

"We must have the wrong house," I said.

Stephanie giggled. "Maybe we do, but I like it!"

"Hello, Chris!" Mr. Jenkins called.

The boy waved and started coming toward us.

"Patti, who is that?" Stephanie whispered.

"The Mitchells' son," Patti said, unloading her suitcase from the van. "Remember, I told you about him."

"You didn't tell me he was so *cute*," Stephanie said. If there's something Stephanie likes better than shopping, it's boys. Lately she's been having crushes on anyone halfway decent with blond hair. Chris was pretty tall, and he had longish blond hair that was kind of wavy. He was cute, but nothing to go crazy over.

"Hi, Mr. Jenkins, Mrs. Jenkins," Chris said. "Hi, Horace." He ruffled Horace's hair.

"Want to play catch?" Horace asked, peering up at Chris through his glasses.

6

"Maybe later," Chris answered. "Hey, Patti." He smiled.

Patti gave him an awkward little wave. "Hi," she said shyly.

"What's up?" asked Chris. "Are you psyched for your birthday?"

Patti nodded. "Yeah, I guess."

Stephanie nudged Patti with her elbow — actually, it was more like she shoved her. Patti practically fell over, but she recovered quickly. "Uh, I feel kind of stiff after being in the car for so long," she said with a little laugh. "These are my friends from Riverhurst."

Stephanie stepped forward. "I'm Stephanie Green. Nice to meet you."

"Yeah, hi," Chris replied. He didn't seem as happy to meet Stephanie as she was to meet him.

"This is Kate, and Lauren," explained Patti.

"I can't believe you all fit in one car," Chris said, glancing inside the minivan.

"Well, it wasn't easy. We had to fast for the last three days," joked Lauren.

Chris laughed. "So, you're ready for dinner, right? We're having a cookout. My parents are out back setting up," he told Patti's parents.

We all picked up our bags and headed into the house. Stephanie hurried to keep up with Chris. She had brought so many clothes for the weekend that her little overnight bag looked like it was going to burst.

"Chris seems like a nice guy," Lauren said to Patti. "Have you known him a long time?"

"Since we were little kids," said Patti. "My mom and his mom went to college together."

"That's neat," said Stephanie. "When did he get so cute?"

Patti shrugged. "I don't know. I never really noticed. You know how when you're friends with someone for a long time, you don't even think about what they look like?"

Lauren pretended to wipe her forehead. "Phew! What a relief! Now I can be ugly and I won't have to worry about you noticing."

"What do you mean, now you can be ugly?" I teased her.

She scowled at me. "I'll get you for that, Beekman."

We walked into the house. It was big, especially considering only three people lived in it. We met Mr. and Mrs. Mitchell, and they told us to put our stuff in the den. We could use that for a changing room, and sleep on the fold-out couches in the living room. The Mitchells were so nice, they made us feel at home the second we stepped through the door. They even told us to take anything we wanted from the refrigerator. I don't think they realized how much we ate at our sleepovers!

That night, however, there was so much food for dinner that even Lauren had to admit she was stuffed. "I can't eat another thing," she told Mrs. Mitchell. "Everything was so delicious."

"Yeah, great meal, Mom," Chris added.

"It's hard to ruin a cookout," Mrs. Mitchell said. "I'll leave the brownies here, in case you get hungry later." She put the plate on the table and went into the house to join the rest of the adults. We were still sitting outside on the deck.

"Like in a few years," Patti joked.

"Seriously," said Chris, shaking his head. "How many hamburgers did I have, anyway?"

"Two," Stephanie answered with a smile. "And one hot dog."

"Patti, remember the time we went to that country fair and watched that hamburger-eating contest?" asked Chris, ignoring Stephanie. "That was gross."

"Those guys tried to shove the whole thing into

their mouths in one bite," Patti explained.

"And they weren't just any burgers, they were *huge*. They had lettuce and tomato and onions on them, too," Chris went on.

"I saw a blueberry-pie-eating contest once," Stephanie said, sitting up in her chair. "Everyone ended up with blue faces — it was hysterical."

"Lauren, have you ever done one of those?" I asked innocently.

She tossed her napkin at me. "Cut it out!"

"Patti, are you still playing baseball?" Chris asked.

"Yeah, Lauren and I play sometimes," Patti answered. "Not as much as I'd like, though."

"I'm playing a lot," said Chris. "I'm on the team at school and I play with a team sponsored by a local store. We have a big game tomorrow afternoon in the city. Maybe you could come watch."

"I don't think so," I said. "I mean, we kind of have the whole day planned." I didn't want to ruin our big surprise for Patti. Plus, once I make a plan, I like to stick with it.

"Well, we don't have the *whole* day planned," Stephanie said sweetly. "Maybe we could drop by for a little while."

"It'd be great if you could," said Chris — but

he was looking straight at Patti when he said it.

The look on Stephanie's face said it all. She was *not* happy. She kept trying to talk to Chris, but the only person he wanted to talk to was Patti!

"Well, maybe," Patti said with a shrug. She hadn't missed Stephanie's expression, either.

"It'll be at the park," Chris said. "Hey, do you still like *The Screamers*? It's on now."

"What's that?" asked Lauren.

"It's an old TV show," I told her. "It's supposed to be really scary, but I've never seen it before. I didn't know you could still watch it."

"It's on every Friday," explained Patti. "That's one thing I miss about the city, having all those weird TV channels that play strange stuff like *The Screamers*."

"Well, let's go inside before we miss it," said Chris, smiling at Patti.

We all got up and went into the living room. Lauren and I sat on the floor — I like to be right up front when I watch TV, partly because I hate wearing my glasses. Stephanie and Patti sat on the couch, and Chris sat right in between them.

He flicked on the TV with the remote, then turned to Patti. "This is going to be great," he said. "Just like old times."

Patti nodded and looked around him at Stephanie. She had her arms folded across her chest and was staring straight ahead at the television.

So far, our big weekend in the city was off to a rocky start!

Chapter
2

After watching *The Screamers,* which wasn't nearly as good as it was cracked up to be, Chris went upstairs to his room. We changed in the den and then stretched out on the fold-out couches. Lauren and Patti were on one, and Stephanie and I were on the other.

"It doesn't feel as if we're anywhere near the city," Lauren said. "It's just as quiet here as it is back home."

"I can't wait until tomorrow," said Patti. "Can you, Stephanie?"

Stephanie sighed. "You know what? I wish we were there right now," she said.

"In your nightshirt?" Lauren giggled. "Now *that* I have to see!"

I studied the train schedule Mr. Mitchell had given us. "Let's take the 9:07 train," I said. "That way we'll be in the city before ten."

"Nine o'clock? You expect us to be ready by nine o'clock?" Stephanie whined.

"I thought you said you wanted to be there right now," I told her. "Unless we get an early start, we won't be able to do all the things we want to do."

"Which are?" Lauren asked.

"Number one, the movie museum. Number two, the science museum. Number three — "

"Lunch," Lauren said.

"Okay." I nodded. "Number four, I guess we want to do some shopping — "

Stephanie sat up in bed. "Definitely! In fact, I could spend all afternoon shopping."

"So what else is new?" Patti teased her.

I made a list of all the things we wanted to do and jotted down the times I thought we should do them. I didn't want us to miss out on anything — we didn't get to the city very often. Then I turned out the light by the couch and lay down. I wanted to go to sleep right away, so I'd be ready for our big day. But I wasn't tired. I was too wound up, thinking about all the things we were going to see and do! I couldn't wait to see that cool restaurant where all the teen stars hung out. I had its address in my wallet — even the address sounded cool.

"Is anyone else awake?" Stephanie asked about half an hour later.

"Yes!" all three of us answered.

She turned on the lamp next to her. "As long as we're all up, we might as well *do* something." She turned on the TV and switched it to the music-video station. "This is a great one!" she said, moving to the music. "Look at his moves!"

"Where did Mrs. Mitchell put those brownies?" asked Lauren, flinging off her sheet and blanket.

Patti looked at me and shrugged. "We should have known we couldn't go to sleep without having a real *sleepover* first."

"I know," I said. "You can take the girls out of Riverhurst, but you can't take — no, that doesn't make sense."

Lauren came back from the kitchen and stood in the doorway. "Kate, quit trying to be poetic and help me find those brownies!"

I got out of bed. "Sorry, I didn't realize it was a national emergency."

"Yeah, a Lauren Hunter Emergency Snack Attack!" added Stephanie, giggling while she danced.

* * *

15

I woke up the next morning to the sound of Saturday-morning cartoons. We had turned on some late-night movie at around midnight and then fallen asleep with the TV on. Stephanie still had the remote in her hand and when she rolled over, she changed the channel to some news show. It was too boring to take, so I got up and switched off the TV.

"Come on, everybody, get up!" I said, shaking Lauren's arm.

"Do we have to?" she groaned.

"Yes, we do. It's already seven-thirty," I told her.

Patti sat up and rubbed her eyes. "We'll never get ready in time."

"Happy birthday!" I cried. "So, who wants to take a shower first? Lauren, why don't you, since your hair takes a long time to dry. Come on, let's get this show on the road."

"Happy birthday, Patti," Lauren muttered as she stumbled across the room toward the bathroom. "I'd love to stick around and talk, but I've been ordered to take a shower."

I touched Stephanie's arm. "Rise and shine, Steph."

She rolled over. "Leave me alone."

It's so hard to have friends who are late sleepers!

16

It drives me crazy, especially when we have big plans. "Stephanie, if we don't leave soon, we won't be able to get in any shopping," I said.

Stephanie flung the covers back from the bed. "Okay, I'm up."

We had to rush to get ready. The Mitchells had gotten fresh bagels from a deli down the street, and we must have eaten them in record time. We didn't see Chris or Horace before we left — they weren't up yet. Then Patti's parents took us to the train station. We bought tickets and agreed to take the 4:14 train back that afternoon.

"Are you sure you have everything you need?" asked Mr. Jenkins.

We all nodded. He had asked us that about twenty times!

"I've got it all in here," I told him, patting my knapsack. We had decided to put everyone's stuff in one bag. Since it was my idea, naturally I had to carry it. That was fine with me. At least that way I'd know it wasn't lost!

"You're sure you have enough money?" Mrs. Jenkins asked.

"Yes, Mom," said Patti.

"Well, I'm glad you bought round-trip tickets, so even if you run out of money you'll still have a way of getting home," Mrs. Jenkins said.

Patti turned to me and rolled her eyes. Parents can be so overprotective. Did they think we were totally irresponsible and stupid? We'd been out on our own before lots of times, even in the city. As long as we stuck together, everything would be fine.

A few minutes later, the train showed up and we climbed on. We found four seats that faced each other, sat down, and looked out the window. The Jenkinses were waving to us as the train pulled away from the station.

"They act as if we're going to Europe or something," said Stephanie as she waved back.

"I don't think you can get there by train," Lauren said with a grin. "Not yet, anyway."

"That reminds me, there's a big transportation exhibit at the science museum," Patti said excitedly. "It has all these cars and planes of the future — Mr. Mitchell was telling me all about it last night at dinner. It sounds fantastic."

"We'll go to the science museum right after the movie museum," I said, winking at Lauren. The plan was actually to take Patti to lunch first — then to the science museum. Since the restaurant was in the same direction, it'd be easy to fool her.

"Do we have to go to the movie museum?" asked Stephanie. "I mean, it's Patti's birthday. We should do what *she* wants to do. Don't you want to buy some new clothes, Patti? Or some new shoes, maybe? I know a *great* shoe store — you'd love it."

Patti shrugged. "Well, maybe."

I took my list out of my jean-jacket pocket. "We're going shopping after the science museum and before the park."

Stephanie took the list out of my hands and quickly scanned it. "Wait a minute. This says shopping, one-thirty to two-thirty. How can you possibly expect us to do anything in an hour? We'll only be able to go to one store!"

Lauren pretended to play a violin. "It's a tragedy."

"We don't have to go to the science musuem," Patti said.

"No, we're definitely going there," I told her. I took the list back from Stephanie and made a few marks on it. "Okay, if we spend half an hour less at the movie museum, we can shop for half an hour more." It's not like me to give up so easily, but I didn't want to argue on Patti's birthday. Besides, I was afraid that if we said anything more, we'd give away the surprise!

Stephanie leaned back in her seat. "That's a *little* better."

"Look out, world," Lauren said with a grin. "Here come the Sleepover Friends!"

Chapter
3

"Wow, that was great," Stephanie said when we walked out of the museum. "I thought it was going to be really boring, but it wasn't."

"I *told* you it would be fun," I said. The movie musuem was every bit as interesting as I had thought it would be. There were props from old movies, lots of cool equipment like cameras and lights, and tons of photographs of stars, stunt people, directors, and Hollywood.

My favorite room, naturally, was the Directors Hall of Fame, with photos of Academy-Award-winning directors. There was some blank space left on it . . . for *my* picture, maybe?

Kate Beekman, the first director to film a movie in outer space, it would say underneath my picture.

I'd be wearing shades in the photo, of course. It can get pretty bright out there near Mars.

"Kate." Lauren was tugging on the sleeve of my jean jacket. "Did you hear what I said or what?"

"No, sorry," I said. "What?"

"I want to put the postcards I bought in your knapsack, okay?" I nodded and turned around so she could slip them into the pocket. "Ready for our fantabulous lunch?" she whispered into my ear as she fiddled with the bag.

"I'm starved," I whispered back.

Stephanie looked over at us and winked. It was time to put the plan into action!

"So, is everyone ready to hit the science museum?" I smiled at Patti.

"Sure, I am," she said. "But if you guys don't want to — "

"No, we do," Lauren said. "My dad says there's an exhibit all about animal rights." Lauren had gotten involved in a big animal rights protest at school a few weeks back when we were supposed to dissect frogs for science class. She had really stood up for the poor slimy things! I was proud of her for doing it.

"Stephanie, are you sure you want to go?" asked

Patti. That's Patti — she thinks about everyone else first, even when it's *her* birthday!

"Oh, I can't *wait*," Stephanie said excitedly. She linked her arm through Patti's, and they walked down the wide stone steps. "I bet it'll be even better than this place!"

I frowned at her back. Science is Stephanie's least-favorite subject. She was going to give the whole thing away!

We went down to the sidewalk and found the bus stop where we could catch the uptown express. The restaurant was way uptown, and so was the museum, so we'd be able to keep Patti in the dark a little while longer.

I checked the bus schedule the Mitchells had given us. "There should be a bus in four minutes. We'd better get our money ready. It's a dollar each." I unzipped the knapsack, grabbed everyone's wallets, and handed them out.

"You have to have exact change," Stephanie said, pocketing four quarters. "They won't take any bills." She pointed to the dollar bill in my hand.

"I know that," I said, shoving the bill back into my wallet. Actually, I hadn't, but I wasn't going to let Stephanie know that. I hated not knowing the right places to go or the right things to do. Being in the city was so new to me. Half the time I couldn't figure out whether we were heading uptown or downtown!

"Here comes the bus!" Stephanie cried. "Does everyone have enough change?"

"Yup, I'm loaded," said Lauren, handing her wallet back to me. She jingled the change in her hand.

I stuffed everyone's wallets back into the knapsack just as the bus pulled up. There were a lot of people trying to get onto it, and all of them were pushing each other, the same way the boys in our class act when it's time for lunch. We were the last ones in line. I hoped there would be enough room on the bus for us!

We were just about to get on when a girl standing over to my left yelled, "It's *her*!"

Stephanie and I turned to look at her. "Who's her?" asked Stephanie.

"I don't know," I said. "It must be some celebrity."

But the girl was looking straight at me! "It's you!" she cried. "I don't believe it! Look, everybody, it's Sarah Spinney!"

"There sure are a lot of crazy people in the city," I said to Stephanie, shaking my head.

She said something back, but I couldn't hear it — there was a big roar all of a sudden, and then a puff of black smoke.

We whirled around just in time to see the bus taking off down the street. Talk about express — it was really moving!

I looked around quickly. Lauren and Patti were nowhere in sight!

"Oh, my gosh! Stop that bus!" Stephanie shouted, waving her hand in the air as she sprinted up the sidewalk after it.

She's a good runner, but I knew we didn't have much hope of catching it. She came back a minute later, completely out of breath. "I can't believe it," she panted. "We missed the bus! We're going to miss having lunch with them and everything."

"Stephanie, it's a lot worse than that," I told her frantically. "I have all the money, remember?"

Stephanie put her hands over her face. "What are we going to do? What are *they* going to do?"

I was trying to calm down and think of a plan when I felt a tap on my shoulder. "Miss Spinney, may I *please* have your autograph?" It was the girl who'd distracted me before. She held out a pencil and a pad of paper.

"I am not this Spinney person, okay?" I told her.

"And thanks a lot for making me miss my bus!"

The girl looked startled. Then she turned to her friend and said, "Those stars are all the same, they're all snobs. Let's get out of here."

"Yeah, well, if she's such a star, how come she's taking the bus?" her friend added as they walked away.

"I'm not taking the bus," I said under my breath. "That's the whole point!"

"Don't worry, Kate, we'll think of something." Stephanie said, pacing back and forth on the sidewalk.

"We'd better," I said. "And fast!"

❖ ❖ ❖ ❖ ❖ ❖

I have to take over telling this part of the story, now that Kate and Stephanie have *deserted* us in the middle of the city.

We climbed onto the bus, dropped our change into the box, and walked back to grab the only seats left, which were near the middle.

"It feels good to sit down," Patti said, sliding into the window seat. "Wait a second — how come Kate and Stephanie are still outside?" She pointed out the window.

"There're still a lot of people trying to get on," I said. "They probably got pushed out of the way."

"I forgot how crowded it can be in the city! We never have to fight to get onto a bus in Riverhurst," said Patti.

I looked up at the front of the bus so I could wave to Kate when she got on. But instead of seeing Kate, I saw the door closing!

"Patti, is it me or are we moving?" I said, standing up. Just as I did, the bus driver pulled out into traffic with a jerk, and I practically fell onto the man sitting behind us.

"They didn't get on!" Patti gasped. She banged on the window, trying to get Kate and Stephanie's attention. "I can't believe it — this is what happened the last time we were here!"

The last time we'd visited the city together, Patti had gotten on a bus without me and Kate (Stephanie and Kate were fighting at the time, so Stephanie wasn't with us). On the same trip, someone had taken *my* suitcase instead of theirs. All in all, it was *not* a successful trip. And now it looked as if we were off on an even worse one!

I ran up to the front of the bus. "Excuse me, sir — "

"Back of the white line," the bus driver grumbled.

I moved back a few steps. "Excuse me, but you

27

have to stop the bus, right now!" I told him.

He pointed above his head at something. I didn't understand what he was trying to tell me.

"Can't you *please* stop? Our friends didn't get on," I explained.

He didn't say anything. He just kept pointing up over his head. Finally, I saw what he was pointing at: a sign that read, DO NOT TALK TO THE DRIVER WHILE THE BUS IS IN MOTION. "Give me a break," I muttered.

I waited until the next stoplight. Then I said, as politely as I could, "I'm sorry to bother you, but my friend and I need to get off this bus right now. Can you open the door?"

The bus driver shook his head. "It's an express. We only make scheduled stops."

"Can't you just pull over and let us out? We won't tell anyone."

"Nope. Company policy," he replied. "What if everyone wanted me to do that? Wouldn't be an express bus." The light turned green, and he floored the accelerator so we took off with a jerk again.

So much for the sign that read, YOUR BUS DRIVER, COURTEOUS, PROFESSIONAL, AND PROMPT! He was way too prompt, if you ask me — he didn't even wait for everyone to get on the bus. And courteous? Ha!

I walked back to my seat. "He won't stop," I told Patti.

"Why not?" she asked.

"He's a grouch," I said. "I guess we'll just have to get off at the next stop, whenever that is." I glanced out the window at the street signs flying by. "At the rate he's going, we should be in another state by then!"

About two minutes later, the bus screeched to a stop. Patti and I jumped up and ran to the front to get off. As I walked past the bus driver, he said, "Have a nice day, girls!"

At the bottom of the steps I turned around and stuck out my tongue at him. He slammed the doors shut, and the bus roared away down the street.

Patti cracked up laughing. "I can't believe you did that!" she said.

"I know, I know. That was totally childish, but I couldn't help it!" I said. "He was such a jerk. Are *all* the bus drivers around here like him?"

We walked to the corner and waited for the light to change so we could cross the street. "No. Actually, I always thought they were pretty nice," said Patti.

"Well, our next one better be," I said. We crossed over and waited at the bus stop for the next downtown express. Fortunately, we weren't waiting for very long before we saw a bus coming down the street. "Is that the right one?" I asked Patti as it pulled up in front of us.

"Yeah, it's the number 19 — we came up on 18," she said.

"Great!" I reached into my jeans pocket for some change, but it was empty. "That's funny, I had a lot of quarters this morn — "

"Lauren, we don't have any money!" Patti cried, interrupting me.

I couldn't believe it. She was right! Kate had all of our money. I groaned loudly. All I had in my pocket was a torn ticket stub from the stupid movie museum. I threw the ticket stub into a trashcan on the street. It was all Kate's fault for making us go there in the first place!

"It looks like *we're* going to miss the bus this time," Patti said as the bus doors opened and the driver peered out at us.

"Do you think she'll take an IOU?" I asked Patti.

✦ ✦ ✦ ✦ ✦ ✦

Chapter 4

"Are you *sure* they're not still here somewhere?" I asked Stephanie. We had looked all over the street for Patti and Lauren, but it was pretty obvious they were gone.

"Kate, we've looked everywhere but under the manholes," Stephanie said with a sigh. "They're on that bus!"

I snapped my fingers. "I know what we should do! Let's take a cab after the bus."

"That won't work," Stephanie replied.

"Sure it will! People do it in the movies all the time. We just get in a cab and say, 'Follow that bus!'"

"It might have worked if we'd done it five minutes ago," said Stephanie. "But that bus is long gone!"

"Yeah, but it goes straight up this street, right? How hard could it be to find it?" I asked. Just then another bus pulled up in front of the museum, dropped off passengers, and took off again.

"Kate, there are dozens of buses around. We couldn't find the one they're on. Besides, maybe they already got out and are on their way back here. We'd probably go right by them," Stephanie reasoned.

"There has to be *something* we can do." I looked around the sidewalk. "Maybe we can ask the police to help. Where are they, anyway?"

"I think they're kind of busy," Stephanie replied. "You know, catching criminals."

I threw up my hands. "Well, let's hear *your* bright ideas!"

"I think we should just wait here. They'll come back," she said confidently. "They don't have any money, right? So they'll probably get off at the first bus stop and walk back."

"Wasn't that an express bus?" I asked. "I mean, the first stop could be *miles* from here."

"No, it won't be that far, trust me. Anyway, they're both in good shape, and they're together. Don't worry, they'll be okay," Stephanie assured me.

"Let's go sit on the museum steps — we'll have a good view from there."

I followed her back over to the museum, and we climbed up to the top steps. "This is all my fault," I said. I slung the knapsack off my back and put it on the step below me.

"What are you talking about?" Stephanie sat down on the steps and gazed up at me. "It's not your fault that girl thought you were some celebrity."

"Not that. I'm the one who has everyone's wallets," I said. "I never should have said I'd carry everything."

"We wanted you to!" Stephanie replied. "I didn't want to walk around the city all day with a knapsack. I thought it was great when you offered to do it."

"Well, it was a stupid idea." I sat down beside her and rested my elbows on my knees. I glanced at my watch. "I wonder if they'll be back in time for us to take Patti to lunch?"

"I know. It'll be terrible if Patti doesn't get her birthday party," said Stephanie. "Do you think they'll hold our table for us?" We had a twelve-thirty reservation, and we'd had to make it two weeks in advance because the place was so popular.

"They'd better," I said.

33

"We'll make it," Stephanie said. She stretched out her legs and leaned back on the step behind her. "While we're waiting, I'm going to work on my tan."

"I hope it doesn't get any hotter," I said. It was a late spring day, but it felt more like the middle of summer. The air was really humid, and my sweatshirt was sticking to my back where the knapsack had been. I put my hand over my eyes to shield them from the sun so I could have a clearer view of the sidewalk. I wasn't going to miss Patti and Lauren when they finally came back!

Stephanie flipped her hair over her shoulder. "L."

I added another leg to the body I had drawn hanging in my notebook.

"R," she said.

I added a foot to the leg. "You're in trouble. . . ."

"Well, what is it then?" Stephanie demanded.

"Give up?" I asked her.

She stared at the blanks on the page. "Yes!"

"It's 'heat wave,'" I told her. I filled in the blanks and showed it to her. "You should have guessed an 'a.'"

"I'm sick of this game." She gathered up her

hair again and tried to tie it into a knot. "It's so hot! I wish I had an elastic band or a barrette. Where *are* they? It's taking forever."

"I know." I stood up. We'd been sitting for over an hour, and there was still no sign of Patti and Lauren. "This concrete isn't getting any softer, either," I said.

"Sarah! Sarah Spinney!" a woman's voice rang out.

"Oh, no," I mumbled, sinking back down onto the steps. It was the fourth time so far that someone had confused me with this Sarah person. And I didn't even know who she was!

A woman wearing a flowered dress, a big hat, and high-heeled shoes hurried over to us. "It's really you!" she exclaimed.

"Well, actually it's not," I told her. "You see, I — "

"You were simply terrific," the woman continued. "I saw the show last month, and I told all my friends they simply had to go see you. I've never heard a child sing so well!"

"I'm not Sarah Spinney," I said through gritted teeth. How dare she call me a child!

"Oh, don't be modest — although that is simply

a wonderful quality in a star so young. Would you please sign this for me?" She held out a postcard from the museum.

I looked at Stephanie and shrugged. Since I couldn't convince the woman I wasn't Sarah Spinney, I might as well play along! I scribbled a big flamboyant signature on the postcard and handed it back to her.

"What a lovely child," she murmured. "Thank you, dear! Best of luck in your career!" She gave me a huge smile and finally walked off down the steps.

Stephanie burst out laughing as soon as she was gone. "You sing so well, Kate!" she cried.

I laughed, too. It's common knowledge that I can't sing to save my life. "I guess Sarah is in a musical," I said. "Better her than me!"

"No kidding!" Stephanie said, laughing.

"It's not that funny," I grumbled. I was pretty sick of people confusing me with that "child" star! I tore a piece of paper out of my notebook and wrote I AM NOT SARAH SPINNEY! DON'T BOTHER ASKING! on it. I went over it a few times with a big black marker that I had in my knapsack. Then I propped it up on the steps. I would have attached it to my shirt, only I didn't have any tape!

"What is that?" asked Stephanie, peering around

me to look at the sign. "Kate! Don't do that!"

"Why not?" I put the cap back on the marker.

"It's embarrassing, that's why not," she argued. "Now *everyone* is going to look at us and think we're weird."

I shrugged. "We'll never see these people again. Anyway, I don't want to spend the rest of the day being called Sarah."

"And I don't want to spend the rest of the day looking like an idiot!" Stephanie replied.

"Fine!" I said, scooting over on the steps so I was farther away from her.

"Oh, yeah?" she said.

"Yeah!" I said.

We just sat there for about five minutes. There wasn't anything else we could do. Neither one of us could storm off and leave the other one. We had to stick together, like it or not. The heat was really getting to me. I needed something to drink. My throat felt the way pictures of the Sahara look.

"Stephanie?" I said, turning to face her.

She just looked at me.

"Are you as thirsty as I am?"

She nodded. "I'm hungry, too. I only had half a bagel for breakfast, and it's already twelve forty-five."

I pointed across the street. "Am I seeing a mirage, or is that a coffee shop over there?"

Stephanie jumped to her feet. "Let's go!"

"Wait a second. What are we going to do about Patti and Lauren?" I asked.

"We'll get a booth by the window so we'll be able to watch for them," said Stephanie. "And we can leave a note here, too, just in case we miss them."

"Good idea!" I was glad I had brought my notebook along to take notes at the museum — it had come in handy! I wrote a quick note explaining where we were and put a rock on it so it wouldn't blow away. I hoped no one would take it. We'd only be gone for a little while. Plus, we would still be watching for them.

Stephanie and I didn't apologize for snapping at each other. We just pretended it hadn't happened. I crumpled up the Sarah Spinney sign and tossed it into a trash can on our way to the restaurant. We were both just cranky because we were so hot and thirsty.

That made me think about Lauren. If *we* were hungry, she was probably starving by now!

Stephanie pushed open the door to the coffee shop, and I followed her. A blast of cold air hit us the second we got inside. "I love air-conditioning," she said with a big grin.

A waiter seated us in a booth with a perfect view of the museum. I flipped through the menu, but I already knew what I wanted: a hamburger deluxe — with French fries — and a vanilla milk shake.

Stephanie slapped her menu down on the table. "I'm going to have the cheeseburger deluxe, onion rings, a side salad, and a hot fudge sundae."

"Stephanie, just because we have Lauren and Patti's money doesn't mean we get to spend it!" I said with a laugh.

Stephanie pretended to be shocked. "It doesn't?" she said. "Well, in that case, I'll just have a bowl of chicken noodle soup. Hold the crackers."

We both laughed, then looked out the window across the street. "Maybe by the time our food comes, they'll be here to share it," Stephanie said. I could tell she was worried, but she was trying to be hopeful about things. I was worried, too. But there wasn't much else we could do.

✦ ✦ ✦ ✦ ✦ ✦

Chapter
5

"Patti, you don't have any gum, do you?"

She shook her head. "Nope. It's in Kate's knapsack, along with everything else."

"I think I'm getting a blister," I said. I stopped and rubbed the side of my foot. "I guess I shouldn't have worn my brand-new sneakers, but I didn't know we were going to be doing a walkathon."

"Does it really hurt?" asked Patti.

"It's not too bad," I said. "How much farther is the museum?"

Patti looked up at the street sign on the corner. "About ten blocks, I think. Can you make it?"

We had been walking for over an hour so far. It was very hot and sticky. I'm in pretty good shape because I jog several times a week with my older brother, Roger. If only I hadn't been wearing new shoes! But we had to get back to the museum, and I was still hoping we could take Patti out to lunch. Lunch . . . just thinking about it made my mouth water.

"Sure, I can make it," I told Patti. "I'll just loosen the laces a little." I did that, and we began walking again.

"I hope we'll still have time for all the things we want to do," said Patti. "It's twelve forty-five already."

"Don't worry, we'll have fun." I winced as my foot rubbed against the sneaker. I didn't want to spoil Patti's birthday with my stupid foot problems.

The next block was really crowded. I guess it was a big intersection or something. There was a department store across the street, with lots of cabs lined up in front of it. "What's that?" I asked Patti.

"Blumdorf's. It's the ritziest store in the city," she said.

"Hm." I stopped for a minute and watched people going in and out of the store. "Maybe we should go over there."

"Why?" asked Patti.

"See all those cabs? We could take one to the museum — since Kate will be there waiting for us, she can pay for it."

"Yeah, but what if she's *not* there? We could get in big trouble."

If the cab drivers were anything like the bus drivers, she was probably right! "Well, maybe we could ask to share someone else's cab. I bet some of those rich people would be nice enough to drop us off at the museum," I said.

Patti wasn't interested, though. "I don't think we should share a cab with anyone we don't know. And I'm definitely not going to ask anyone for money!"

She's really shy about going up to strangers. But in this case, I knew she was right. It was dangerous, and stupid, too. We had gotten ourselves into this mess, and we could get ourselves out of it.

"Okay, let's go," I said. We turned and started walking. At the next corner, while we were waiting to cross the street, I suddenly smelled something *wonderful*. I couldn't figure out what it was until I saw a cart on the other side of the street. "Patti, do you smell that?" I took a deep breath.

She nodded. "Honey-roasted peanuts. They're *sooo* good."

We crossed over and walked right past the cart. I stopped for a second and stared longingly at the peanuts. The man at the cart was stirring them around in a big copper bowl with a wooden spoon. "How many?" he asked me.

I looked at the sign on the cart: FRESH HONEY-ROASTED PEANUTS, ONLY $1. Only one dollar more than I had . . . I was about to ask him if he'd give me one to taste when a couple came up and ordered *two* bags. My mouth watered as I watched him scoop the peanuts into the bag. It wasn't fair! Here I was in the city, where there were all these wonderful things to eat, and I couldn't try any of them!

Patti took my arm and gently pulled me away from the cart. "Come on, we're losing time. We'll get some later," she said.

"I don't want them later, I want them now," I complained. Then I got a grip on myself. "I'm sorry, Patti — I get grumpy when I'm really hungry."

"It's okay, I'm hungry, too. We'd better have a good lunch when we find Stephanie and Kate!"

"Oh, we will," I said. "I promise!"

"We'd better hurry," said Patti, pointing up at the sky. There were a couple of big, dark clouds covering up the sun. It was nice that it wasn't so hot anymore, but I didn't want to get stuck in a down-pour on top of everything else.

"Okay, let's speed-walk," I said.

We passed two ice-cream vendors, three pretzel carts, and one hot dog stand before we *finally* saw the museum. "There it is!" I cried. Then there was a big rumbling noise in the sky that sounded suspiciously like thunder.

"Uh-oh!" Patti yelled, and we both started running for the museum.

"Do you see them?" I said. "I don't." It was pretty deserted in front of the museum. It looked like everyone had cleared out so they wouldn't get caught in the storm. Or else they were all eating lunch. . . .

"I don't see them, either," said Patti. We stopped running and stared up at the museum entrance. "There's no one up there."

"Wait — what's that?" I pointed to a piece of paper near the top of the steps.

"It's litter, probably," said Patti with a frown. There was a loud crack, and all of a sudden we were being pelted with raindrops.

"Let's check it out, anyway!" I yelled over the noise of the rain. "Maybe they left us a note!" We took the steps three at a time — it's a good thing we both have long legs. The rain was coming down really hard, and my hair was already soaked.

I picked up the piece of paper, which was underneath a rock. Something had definitely been written on it, but the ink was running all over my hands! It was impossible to read. "Look, Patti! It's a piece of notebook paper. "Maybe Kate left us a note — she brought her notebook, remember?"

Patti shook her head, sending water flying. "Anyone could have that kind of notebook!" she cried.

"Yeah, but I *know* it was Kate."

"So what if it was? We can't read it!" Patti said. There was another clap of thunder, and she yelled, "Let's go inside!"

We sprinted to the museum entrance. I didn't even feel my blister. Actually, the rain felt kind of good — it was cooling me off. We stepped through the doors, expecting to see Kate and Stephanie waiting inside for us.

Instead, there was a security guard. "Can I see your tickets?"

"Oops." I smiled. "I threw mine out. But we were here this morning."

"We're just looking for our friends," Patti explained. She reached into her pocket and pulled out her ticket stub from that morning.

"I can't read this," said the guard, examining the crumpled, wet piece of paper. "It could be from anywhere."

"We swear we were here before," said Patti. "Honest! We just need to look around and see if our friends are here. We got separated and, um, it's an emergency."

The guard simply shook his head. "I can't let you in without tickets."

"But we had them!" I cried. "I bought postcards, and — wait, I can prove it to you. I'll tell you what's in every room here." I probably couldn't, but I had to do something. I took a few steps into the museum and looked around for Kate.

The guard moved so he was standing in front of me. "I'm sorry, girls. I'm going to have to ask you to leave now."

"Can't we just stay until the rain stops?" I asked. Not that I was so sure that was a good idea — the air-conditioning was on full power, and it felt too cold now that I was soaked to the bone. But staying in the museum was our only hope for catching up with Kate and Stephanie. I took a few more steps forward. "We'll just sit on that bench over there and be *really* quiet."

"We won't bother anyone," said Patti.

The guard took both of us by the elbows and escorted us back to the front door. He let go of us long enough to open it, then he gently pushed us out. "Come back when you can afford to, girls," he said.

I was going to stick out my tongue at him, too, but he didn't seem as if he would take it very well. "Now what?" I asked Patti. The rain had let up a lot, so at least we had a chance to dry out.

"Do you have *any* money at all?" she replied.

"I think I have a dime," I said. I reached into the little change pocket in my jeans and pulled it out. "I must have left this in here the last time I wore these. It went through the wash."

"I feel as if I just went through the wash," said Patti. She twisted the bottom of her T-shirt, and water dripped to the ground. Looking at her, I felt a pang of sadness. Here it was, her birthday — it was supposed to be one of the happiest days of the year — and she was soaking wet, broke, and hungry. Suddenly I didn't feel so sorry for myself.

I had to do something to make her birthday better! "How much money do you have?" I asked her.

47

"I have fifteen cents," she said.

"Let's call the Mitchells," I said. "They can meet us here, and then our problems will be over. You know their number, don't you?"

Patti nodded. "But what about Stephanie and Kate?"

"They have the train tickets, so they'll get home eventually," I said. "Don't worry about them. Stephanie knows her way around."

"I think there's a phone booth over there," Patti said. We headed toward the right side of the building, where there were about four phone booths. "Boy, it's going to feel good to put on some dry clothes!"

The first phone I picked up didn't have a dial tone. I wasn't surprised. The way our day was going, I half expected the phone to break in two when I touched it.

The next phone did work. I listened as our last twenty-five cents in the world dropped into it, clanking against all the other change in there. Luckily for us, the Mitchells lived close enough to the city that it wasn't long distance. When their phone started ringing, I turned to Patti and said, grinning, "All right, now we're talking."

"I hope they're not mad at us," she said, looking concerned.

"When we tell them what we've been through, they'll probably take us out to lunch, and then shopping at Blumdorf's!" I said. Then I gave her the thumbs-up sign — Mr. Mitchell had answered the phone!

"Hello, this is the Mitchell residence," he said.

"Mr. Mitchell! This is Lauren, and Patti and I — "

"We can't take your call right now," Mr. Mitchell continued.

"You have to!" I insisted. "See, we're stuck in the city and we — "

"But if you'd like to leave a message with your name, your number, and the time you called, we'll get back to you as soon as possible. Wait for the beep. Thank you."

"It's the answering machine," I told Patti. "What should I say?"

"Anything! Tell them where we are!"

"Hello, this is Lauren, you know, Lauren Hunter, Lauren who's staying at your house? Patti and I are at the movie museum. We lost Kate and Stephanie, and they have all the money, and we don't have our tickets to get home, and it's really hot, only we got caught in a thunderstorm and we're soaked, so could you please bring some clothes for us

49

and — " The machine beeped three times to let me know my thirty seconds were up.

I hung up the phone and shrugged. "Maybe it'll work. Where do you think they are?"

"I think my mom said something about a big flea market," said Patti. "They might be gone for a while."

I reached up and fiddled with the coin-return lever, but nothing came out. Then I checked all the other phones for change, but there wasn't any. I guess someone had been there before me.

Patti leaned over and ruffled her hair with her fingers. "I hope I don't run into anyone I know," she said, wringing out her shirt again.

"Except Kate and Stephanie!" I added. "Where *are* they, anyway?"

"Maybe they thought we were going to meet them at the science musuem. We probably should have stayed on that stupid bus!" Patti wailed.

I bit my lip. "Patti, if it makes you feel any better, I know they're not at the science museum."

She looked at me, confused. "What?"

"We weren't going to the science museum. We just told you that," I said. "We were going to take you out to lunch. It was supposed to be a surprise." Some surprise! So far, the only surprise had been that

Kate and Stephanie sent us off on the bus by ourselves.

But instead of looking upset, Patti smiled. "Really? You guys are great." She paused. "So why don't we just meet them at the restaurant?" She glanced at her watch.

I rubbed my forehead. "The thing is, I don't know where the restaurant is. Kate has all the information about it."

"Well, what's it called?"

I shook my head. "I don't remember that, either. Kate was in charge of the whole thing."

"Oh." Patti nodded.

"We *will* take you out for a birthday lunch, I promise," I said. "It'll just have to be tomorrow, I guess."

"So, they're not here, they're not at the science museum, and they're not at the Mitchells'. No one's at the Mitchells'." Patti looked around the block and started chewing her fingernails. "Now what?"

◆ ◆ ◆ ◆ ◆ ◆

Chapter
6

"Do you want the last bite, or can I have it?" Stephanie asked, her fork poised over our piece of apple pie à la mode.

I sat back in the booth and put my fork on the table. "Go ahead — I'm stuffed!" I hadn't been very hungry to begin with, maybe because I was so worried. Also, maybe because I'd been so hot.

Stephanie licked her lips. "The food here is pretty good. I mean, it's not going to get written up in *Teen Topics*, and there aren't cute guys crawling all over the place, but — wait a second, hold that thought." She sat up straight and quickly wiped her mouth with a napkin. "Gorgeous hunk at twelve o'clock," she whispered. "Act casual."

Stephanie was facing the door, so it was impossible for me to look at the hunk without being obvious. I decided to wait for him to walk past our table. Stephanie had this look on her face as if to say, "Don't even try to talk to us, we are so cool." She sipped her water and looked up at the guy out of the corner of her eye as he walked by. It wasn't just one guy — it was a whole group — and they sat in the booth right behind Stephanie. From what I could see, they were all pretty cute.

"Switch seats with me," Stephanie whispered.

I shook my head. "We don't have time to hang out, anyway," I told her. "We have to keep on the lookout for Patti and Lauren, remember?"

"I can see just as well out the window from your side of the table as from mine," Stephanie argued in a low voice.

"Yeah, but if you sit over here, you won't look anywhere but over there," I whispered, gesturing toward the boys' booth.

"I will, too!" said Stephanie. Just then there was a loud crack of thunder. The lights in the coffee shop dimmed for a second, then went back on.

"Oh, no!" I looked out the window at the museum. "What if Patti and Lauren get caught in this storm?"

"Look — it's starting to rain!" Stephanie said.

A few seconds later it was raining so hard that people were scurrying into doorways all along the street. I could barely see across to the museum because the coffee shop window was blurry with water.

Suddenly one of the guys turned around and tapped Stephanie on the shoulder. "Excuse me, can we borrow your salt? We don't have a — hey," he said, looking at me for the first time, "aren't you Sarah Spinney?" He grinned. "Wow, I can't believe it. Hey, guys, check it out — Sarah Spinney's over here."

I should have held onto my dumb sign after all! Now all the boys at the table were looking at me.

Stephanie scooted over to one side and put her legs up on the seat. "Hi, I'm Stephanie," she said.

"Is she your friend?" one boy asked her, pointing to me.

Stephanie smiled. "Yes, she is."

"What's the matter, don't you talk?" another boy asked me.

"Sure, I talk, but I'm not Sarah Spinney," I said.

"Come on, get real," the first boy said. "I've seen your picture all over the place."

I looked at Stephanie. She was winking at me. I guess she was trying to tell me something, but she looked like she had something in her eye.

"No, really — I'm not. I don't even know who she is," I said.

"Are you trying to be incognito or something?" another boy asked. "So the newspapers don't get a picture of you wearing sweats and pigging out?"

"What's wrong with wearing a sweatshirt?" I said.

"What Sarah means is, just because she's a star, she doesn't have to dress up all the time, does she?" Stephanie said with a sweet smile.

I glared at Stephanie. She was pretending I was Sarah just so she could get to know the gorgeous hunk!

"So, what do you two do for fun?" the cutest boy asked Stephanie.

Here we go, I thought. I leaned back with a sigh and looked out the window. But suddenly I saw something that made me sit up.

"Stephanie, look — it's Patti!" I cried, jumping out of the booth.

"Where?" she asked.

"Over there on the steps!" I said. "Let's go!"

"*What* is going on?" asked one of the boys.

"We'll explain later," said Stephanie. "We have to run!"

"She's probably trying to escape some photographer!'' another boy added as Stephanie and I dashed to the door.

It was still pouring, but we had no choice. "Ready, Steph?" I zipped up the knapsack and held it over our heads.

She nodded, and we took our first step forward — and stopped. I couldn't move. Someone was holding on to the back of my sweatshirt! "Look, I told you, I'm not Sarah Spinney!" I said, whirling around, expecting to see one of the guys holding out a menu of me to autograph.

It was the waiter. "No one stiffs me with the check," he said, frowning.

"Excuse me?" I said.

"He means we have to pay before we can leave," Stephanie explained.

"We can't!" I said.

The waiter folded his arms across his chest and glared at me.

"No, no, we have the money, it's not that," I said. "We have to go right now! It's an emergency."

"Just tell us what we owe!" said Stephanie.

The waiter took his pad and pen out of his pocket. He flipped through the pad, looking for our check. "What did you have again?" he asked us.

I threw up my hands. "You're the waiter!"

He glared at me.

"Kate, give me the money — you go across the street and get Patti and Lauren," Stephanie said. "I'll be right there."

"Okay," I said, giving her the knapsack. The rain had let up slightly, so I had a clear view of the museum. Now I didn't see anyone who looked at all like Patti or Lauren, but I rushed over anyway. I had to wait for the light to change so it took a minute.

At the base of the steps, a family was gathered underneath an umbrella. There were a few kids hanging out under the museum roof's edge. That was it. Patti had vanished!

Stephanie came up beside me. "Where are they?"

"I don't know. I thought I saw Patti right around here." I turned all the way around, but still no Patti.

"You must have confused her with someone else," said Stephanie.

"I don't think so. She's wearing that bright blue shirt, remember? I saw it. That's how I recognized her."

"Lots of people probably have that shirt," said Stephanie. "Anyway, aren't you supposed to wear glasses? Your vision isn't exactly perfect."

I put my hands on my hips. "Do you want to find them or not?"

"Of course, I do!" Stephanie looked upset. "I'm just saying maybe they *weren't* here yet."

"Well, it was your idea to leave and go eat in the first place," I grumbled.

"It was not, it was yours!" argued Stephanie.

Eating lunch hadn't done much to improve our moods! "I'm sorry," I said. "It was both of ours, okay?" I snapped my fingers. "I know — let's see if the note is still here!"

We ran up the steps to the place we'd been sitting earlier.

"It's gone," said Stephanie. "Maybe they got it!"

"Or maybe it blew away — or floated away," I said.

"Just in case they did read it, I'll go back and check the coffee shop to make sure they're not there, okay?" Stephanie offered.

I raised one eyebrow at her. "Are you sure that's why you're going back there?"

"Yes!" she said. "I'll be right back."

While I waited for Stephanie, I asked a couple of people if they had seen two girls. Everyone said yes — they had seen several girls, in fact. But they couldn't remember what any of them looked like! I wished I had a picture of Patti and Lauren so I could conduct a real search, the way they do on television.

Stephanie came back right away, as promised. No one in the coffee shop had seen two girls like Patti and Lauren, either. We decided to go into the museum and see if anyone knew anything.

"Hi," I said to the security guard just inside the front door. "Can I ask you something?"

"It's two dollars for children under twelve," he replied.

I shook my head. "No, I've already been in today. I don't want to go into the museum — I'm looking for some friends."

"Who isn't?" the guard said. He chuckled.

"Listen, this is serious," said Stephanie. "We got split up from our friends and we absolutely *have* to find them. We thought we saw them outside a minute ago, but now they're gone. Has anyone come in here recently?"

"Only about two hundred people," the guard said. "But describe them — I have a pretty good memory. Used to be a detective on the force, you know."

"Good, maybe you can help us, then," I said. "Okay, they're ten years old — actually, one is eleven. They're both kind of tall for their age. One has light brown hair, and the other has dark brown hair."

The security guard made a *tsking* noise with his tongue. "That's not much to go on."

"I'm not finished!" I said. "One is wearing a bright blue T-shirt, I mean, really bright blue. The other has on jeans and new white sneakers — "

"Wait a second." The guard scratched his head. "Bright blue, you say? As a matter of fact, there was a girl here just a few minutes ago with a shirt like that. She and her friend got caught in the rain and they wanted to dry out in here. And, now that I think about it, they did say something about being separated from their friends. But I told them, no ticket, no loitering!" He smoothed the front of his uniform.

"So you're saying they were here just a few minutes ago?" Stephanie asked excitedly.

"I can't believe we missed them!" I said, pacing back and forth on the floor.

"They have to be outside *somewhere*," said Stephanie. "They couldn't have gone far."

"Let's go outside — maybe we can still catch them," I said.

"Good luck!" the guard called as we went out the door.

We walked all the way around the museum, but we didn't see them anywhere. "How did they vanish into thin air so quickly?" asked Stephanie.

"I don't know." I said. "Look, there are some pay phones. Why don't we call the Mitchells — maybe they've heard from them."

"Good idea!" Stephanie grabbed some change from her wallet. "Here, call Directory Assistance for the number."

"I wrote it down in my notebook," I said.

She laughed and handed me the notebook. "I should have known! Kate, do you ever forget *any*-thing?"

"No," I said. "Not that I know of, anyway. Okay, here it is." I put a quarter in the phone and dialed the Mitchells' number. Someone picked it up on the second ring. "Hi, this is Kate!" I said before they could say anything.

"Hello, this is the Mitchell residence," a voice replied. "We can't take your call right now."

"It's the machine," I told Stephanie. I didn't

know what to say. I didn't want to worry everybody, but if we couldn't find Patti and Lauren, it *was* something to worry about.

I decided to leave a message that would help Patti and Lauren if they called the Mitchells later, if they could — they might not even have enough money to call! I explained that we were waiting at the movie museum for them, wondering where they were . . . and I added that it was one-thirty. I hoped the Jenkinses wouldn't flip out when they heard we weren't together. We'd see them soon enough, and then we could explain everything!

I hung up the phone and said, "Now what do we do?"

"They're probably still around here somewhere," Stephanie said. "It's only been ten minutes since the guard saw them. They're probably walking around the museum, just like us. If we stay in one place, they'll *have* to find us. It's only logical."

I almost burst out laughing. Stephanie, being logical? This was a first! "Are you sure you don't want to hang out here so you can see your gorgeous hunk again?" I teased her.

She grinned. "Well, if he happens to walk by, I won't mind."

"Okay." I sighed. "Let's go back to the front

steps. At least we'll have a good view of the coffee shop."

"Look on the bright side," said Stephanie as we sat down on the wet concrete. "We *could* be in Lauren's and Patti's shoes!"

"I almost wish we were," I said. "Then I wouldn't feel so guilty!"

◆ ◆ ◆ ◆ ◆ ◆

Chapter
7

Patti and I stood by the phone for a few minutes after we called the Mitchells. We didn't know what to do. Patti had bitten all of her fingernails, and it looked as if she were about to start on her fingers, so I had to think of something fast. I'd looked at every store on the street, trying to think where Stephanie and Kate would have gone.

Sometimes the fact that Riverhurst has only a few places to hang out bugs me, but right then I would have given anything to be spending our Saturday there, at the good old Riverhurst Mall, looking at the same clothes we had seen in Just Juniors the week before, then ordering our usual pizza at the Pizza Palace. . . .

Well, it was no use thinking about what *could*

have been. We had to deal with the situation we were in now. "Patti, see that place over there called Lowe's Travel?" I said.

She nodded.

"It looks like they're open. Maybe they can help us," I said. "See that sign in the window, TRAVELERS ASSISTANCE? We're travelers, right? And we need assistance. It's worth a shot."

"Okay." Patti shrugged. She seemed to have given up hope. What a terrible birthday she was having.

We walked across the street and into the travel agency. "Hello," the woman at the desk nearest the door greeted us. "May I help you?"

"Hi. I hope so," I said. "We'd like some travelers assistance." I figured the more important I made it sound, the more likely they would be to help us. "It's an emergency, actually."

"Mr. Harmon handles that area," the woman said, smiling politely. She swiveled around in her chair. "He's on the phone right now, but I'll ask him to help you as soon as he's through. Please, have a seat." She gestured toward some chairs and a coffee table piled high with brochures.

"I can't believe they ask you to wait when it's an emergency," I complained as we sank into the comfortable chairs. "It's a good thing this isn't a hospital."

"I don't care — it feels so good to sit down!" Patti stretched out her legs. "I wish my clothes would dry."

"I know," I said, peeling my jeans away from my legs. "There's nothing worse than sitting around in wet clothes. Except maybe sitting around in wet clothes *and* being incredibly hungry."

The woman from the front desk walked past carrying a cup of coffee. "Help yourselves, girls — it's fresh brewed," she said, pointing toward a coffeepot on a table a few feet away. She went back to her desk.

I looked at Patti. "Have you ever had coffee before?"

"Sometimes I have a sip of my dad's. I don't really like it," she said.

"I don't think I've ever tried it," I said. "But there's a first time for everything, right?" I went over to the table and poured some coffee into a cup. I added four packets of sugar and stirred in a lot of that artificial creamer stuff that looks like flour. It smelled pretty good — maybe it would be just like coffee ice cream.

I sat back down next to Patti and opened a brochure about the Bahamas. "I'd love to go to a tropical island, wouldn't you?" I asked her. "Imagine if we were there right now, swimming in the ocean, collecting shells, playing volleyball on the beach . . ."

"I wish!" Patti said, resting her head on the back of the chair.

I took my first sip of coffee. What a shock! It was all I could do to keep from spitting it onto the carpet!

"Yuck!" I cried when I finally managed to swallow it. "Patti, why didn't you warn me?"

"Is it that bad?" she asked.

I held out the cup. "Here, taste it."

"No, thanks. I think I'll have some water."

"That was the most disgusting thing I have ever tasted," I said, making a face. "I can't believe people actually *drink* that." So much for making a meal out of coffee.

"Girls, Mr. Harmon can see you now," the receptionist told us.

I dumped my coffee cup into the trash on the way to Mr. Harmon's desk. "Just be really innocent and pathetic," I said softly to Patti before we sat down. "Maybe if we cry, he'll give us money for lunch."

"I understand you need some travelers assistance," Mr. Harmon said. "May I see your travelers association identification card?"

"Our what?" I said.

"The card that identifies you as members of the travelers association," Mr. Harmon explained.

I glanced at Patti. "Oh, *that*," she said. "We, ah, don't have it with us."

Mr. Harmon tapped his desk with his fingernails. "I suppose I could get your ID number from the computer. What name is it listed under, please?" He pulled his chair over in front of the computer.

If only we could be sure one of our names was on the list! "Uh, it's under my father's name," I lied. "Robert Smith."

Mr. Harmon punched the name into his computer. "Residence, please?"

"Uh . . . San Francisco, California," I said. It was a big city. There had to be a Robert Smith.

"I have several listings. What's the street address?"

I panicked. I didn't know the names of any streets in San Francisco — I had never been there. Our friend Hope used to live there, but that didn't help much. Maybe I should have used her father's name, I thought. It was too late now.

68

Mr. Harmon looked at me and raised his eyebrows. "Street address?"

"Oh, sorry, I didn't hear you. It's, ah, Thirteenth Street," I said. Most big cities had numbered streets — at least I hoped so.

Mr. Harmon shook his head. "There's no Robert Smith on Thirteenth Street. Sorry."

"But I swear, my father is a member," I said. "He talks about it all the time. He travels a lot on business."

"Is that so? Well, you probably just misunderstood the name of the organization he belongs to. We only handle travelers association members who hold current memberships and carry ID cards." Mr. Harmon stood up. "It's been nice talking to you."

I slowly got to my feet, partly because my legs were so tired, and partly because I didn't want to leave yet.

"Excuse me, Mr. Harmon," Patti said. "We weren't exactly telling you the truth just now."

He looked at her over the top of his wire-rimmed glasses. "Oh?"

"No," she said. "But we're in trouble, and we need your help. We saw the sign for travelers assistance and we thought it meant everybody, so we came in."

"Yes, I suppose that sign is misleading," Mr. Harmon said, sitting back down. "Still, I can't help you unless —"

"I know, unless we're members," I said.

"But maybe you could help us just a little," Patti continued. "See, we're only here for the day, and something happened, and we don't have any money."

"Did someone take your bags?" Mr. Harmon looked genuinely concerned.

"Not exactly," I said. "Our friend Kate has all our money."

"Are you saying she took it from you?"

"No, we got separated," said Patti. "And now we can't find her and we haven't had anything to eat all day, and we've walked all over the place looking for them, and Lauren has a bad blister so she can't walk much further."

Mr. Harmon shook his head. "I tell all my clients to wear sensible shoes when they travel. It's a shame to ruin a perfectly good trip just because your feet hurt!"

I frowned at him. This was assistance?

"The other thing you should always do when you travel is put some emergency money inside your sock," Mr. Harmon went on. "Say, ten dollars. That

70

way you'll never be stuck. Of course, traveler's checks are the best way to go."

"Mr. Harmon, it's your wife on line two!" the receptionist announced.

"Excuse me, girls." Mr. Harmon grinned at us. "Help yourselves to some coffee."

I turned to Patti. "I guess we might as well take off, unless you want to hear the rest of the lecture on travel tips."

Patti nodded. We stood up and walked toward the door.

"Girls?" the receptionist said when we passed her desk. "I wasn't eavesdropping, but it's a small office and, well, I heard about your problem. I'd like to help."

Patti and I practically crawled over to her desk. I felt like a castaway on a deserted island who had just seen her first message in a bottle. "Did you say you'd help us?" I asked.

"I'd like to, if I can," she said with a smile. "I do have two tokens I can give you for the bus or the subway. Would that help?"

We both nodded eagerly. "We know we can meet up with our friends at the train station later this afternoon," Patti explained. "We know what train we're taking back to the house where we're staying — we just need to get to the station!''

"And we know the people we're supposed to take the train with will be on time,'' I said. Kate was probably calculating the minutes even as I spoke, so she would be at the station exactly ten minutes before the train left.

"Good.'' The receptionist smiled and handed us two tokens. "Well, this way you'll be able to get there without walking across town again.'' Then she opened the top drawer of her desk and pulled out a brown paper bag. "I always keep some of these around for long afternoons.'' She pointed behind her at Mr. Harmon and rolled her eyes. "Anyway, it's not much, but it's yours,'' she said, handing me the bag.

When I opened it, my eyes practically popped out of my head. There were two *king-size* candy bars inside! "Thanks!'' I said. I took them out and showed them to Patti.

Her face lit up instantly. "You saved our lives,'' said, staring at the candy bars.

"I wish I could do more,'' said the receptionist. "Tell you what — I get off work at five o'clock. If you still haven't met up with your friends, come back here and I'll take you home.''

"Okay. Thanks,'' I said. She was so nice! She

didn't know anything about us, and she was going out of her way to help. "Can I have one of your business cards?" I asked her. I wanted to write her a thank-you note when I got home. Two tokens and two candy bars might not sound like much, but right then, it was as good as winning the million-dollar lottery to me and Patti!

She gave me one of her cards. "Thanks, Ms. Hannaford," I said.

"Please call me Becky!" She smiled. "Well, good luck to you two. I hope you have a fun visit!"

"Thanks," said Patti. She sounded strange, as if she were in a trance. She kept staring at the candy bars.

We went outside and waved good-bye to Becky through the window. "What a nice woman," I said.

Patti stared at me blankly.

"What's wrong?" I asked her.

She pointed at the candy bars. "Food. Now."

That was a switch. Usually *I'm* the one who can't think about anything except food. "Okay, okay! Let's go sit on the steps over there and eat," I said. "Maybe Stephanie and Kate will come back from wherever they are."

We sat down on the museum steps, near the bottom, and each of us took a candy bar. I unwrapped mine and took a huge bite. I had never tasted anything so wonderful in my entire life. It was better than a whole pan of Kate's chocolate-marshmallow fudge, or Mrs. Green's peanut butter-chocolate chip cookies. . . . I glanced at my watch. It was two-thirty. I had never gone so long without eating before.

I looked over at Patti and grinned. She had a tiny smear of chocolate on her face, and she looked extremely happy. "Happy birthday," I said, knocking my candy bar against what was left of hers.

"Thanks," she said. "Maybe you'd like to give me my present now?"

"Yeah? And what would that be?" I asked, taking another bite.

"The rest of your candy bar!" she said.

"Patti, you're one of my best friends in the whole world, and I think you're terrific, and I wish you only the best on your birthday," I said, "but forget it!" I popped the rest of the candy bar into my mouth. Friendship only goes so far!

✦ ✦ ✦ ✦ ✦ ✦

Chapter 8

"What time is it?" asked Stephanie.

"Twenty after two," I said with a sigh. I saw someone looking at me with a grin of recognition, and I turned the other way.

"What's your problem?" said Stephanie.

"It's another Sarah Spinney fan," I said out of the corner of my mouth. We'd only been back on the museum steps for half an hour, and already four more people had come up to me, alias Sarah Spinney. I'd always heard stars say that being a celebrity was a problem, but I'd never believed them — until that day! If I really were Sarah Spinney, I wouldn't leave the house without a good disguise. And maybe a bodyguard.

"Ignore them," Stephanie said. Easy for her to

say — she wasn't the one everyone was staring at! "Kate, I don't think Lauren and Patti are going to show up here again, do you?"

"Well . . . I guess I kind of doubt it," I said. "I mean, it's been a long time now since the guard saw them. And we don't even know if that *was* them."

"I know. Look, they know we're taking the 4:14 train back to the Mitchells', right? So they'll be at the train station. In the meantime, I think we should try to salvage something out of the day." Stephanie took her brush out of the knapsack and started brushing her hair.

I gave her a skeptical look. "What did you have in mind? Flirting with more boys at the coffee shop?"

"No! Something better," she replied. "It's the hour we were supposed to spend shopping, remember?"

I groaned.

"Come on, Kate. It'll be fun! Don't you want to see the new summer stuff? And there's that great toy store, too," Stephanie said.

"But, Steph, everyone's going to be calling me Sarah," I said. "At least here I can hide, sort of."

"I have an idea!" Stephanie cried. "I know a great store called Hats Off to You."

"So?" I asked, confused.

Stephanie sighed with frustration. "Don't you pay *any* attention when you watch all those old detective movies? If you don't want anyone to recognize you, you wear a big floppy hat and sunglasses."

"Great idea," I said. "But are you sure we shouldn't wait a little while longer for them?"

Stephanie stood up and slung the knapsack over her shoulder. "If we wait any longer it'll be four o'clock, and we'll miss the whole day. Come on, let's go."

I stood up, feeling a bit reluctant. "I don't know, Steph. Aren't you worried about them?"

Stephanie shook her head. "Patti's the smartest girl in our whole class, and Lauren has lots of common sense. They'll be fine." She grabbed my arm. "It's not going to do any good to sit around worrying."

"I know," I said. "But I feel so helpless! I feel like the second we leave here, they're going to show up again. Then they're really going to think we deserted them."

"Kate, if they haven't come back here yet, they're not going to. They obviously have another plan. So . . ."

"We should go shopping?" I said. The idea of us having fun and spending money while Patti and

Lauren were wandering around, broke, seemed wrong to me. But Stephanie did have a point — there really wasn't much we could do. And they *would* be at the train . . . wouldn't they?

"Yes, we should," said Stephanie. "We can buy presents for them, to make up for the lousy day they've had."

I was standing there trying to decide what to do when a couple walked up to us. "Excuse me, but aren't you Sarah Spinhead?" the woman asked me.

Stephanie giggled, and I grabbed her arm. "Let's go get that hat," I said, pulling her down the steps beside me.

"Miss Spinhead, please!" the woman called after us. "I just want your autograph for my daughter!"

"It's Spinney, not Spinhead!" I called over my shoulder.

"Boy, talk about your temperamental stars," Stephanie said as we crossed the street. "She's lucky you didn't punch her out!"

"It's tough being a celebrity. Seriously!" I said. "And I'm not even a real one."

"Yet," added Stephanie. "Okay, first thing we'll do is get the hat and sunglasses. Then we'll hit Mixed Mode, Leland's, and, oh, we have to go to Kicks to look at shoes, plus there's this store with really great sweats, and . . .''

Stephanie kept talking, but I kind of tuned her out. I couldn't believe I was going to the biggest shopping district in the city with the biggest shopper in the world. I'd be lucky if we made the 4:14 train the *next* day!

❖ ❖ ❖ ❖ ❖ ❖

"Look at those pants!" I leaned back on the step behind me and laughed. "Can you imagine wearing those to school?"

Patti and I were sitting on the steps of the museum, watching everyone walk by. We had seen so many different outfits that I felt as if I could write an article for *Teen Topics* on the latest urban fashions!

"Only if I wore a paper bag over my head," Patti added. The pants we were talking about were skin tight, and they had bright orange and pink flowers on them. They looked good on the 'woman wearing them, but I think she was a model. You'd have to be gorgeous to get away with clothes that ugly!

"Here comes the Wayne Miller look-alike contest winner," I said. Wayne Miller is the grossest boy in school.

"I can't believe it — he looks just like Wayne," Patti whispered as the boy walked past us.

"They were probably separated at birth," I said. "Yuck! How horrible — there are *two* Wayne Millers in this world."

"I like that woman's haircut." Patti pointed at a woman with short blonde hair sleeked back from her forehead. "She reminds me of someone on TV."

"Yeah, I know who you mean but I can't remember her name," I said.

Patti jabbed her elbow in my ribs. "Look at that guy's haircut!"

We both stared at this tall guy as he walked in front of us. His hair was sticking straight up on his head, one side of it was dyed green, and in the back it was shaved into diagonal patterns! "I think he's your type," I said to Patti.

"He looks like he's from another planet," she said. "I think we should tell the guys in our class to do their hair that way. Can you imagine Henry with that haircut?" Patti cracked up.

Henry Larkin is sort of Patti's boyfriend. They sit next to each other in class, and they've liked each other for as long as I can remember.

I was thinking about Henry, and whether or not I'd ever have a boyfriend, when all of a sudden this kid came zooming up in front of us on his skateboard. He was trying really hard to be cool, doing all these fancy moves, when he ran right into the wall.

I looked at Patti and rolled my eyes as if to say, "What an idiot." She nodded.

"Hey," the boy said, walking over in front of us. Actually, he *was* kind of cute. His hair was a little long, and it was cut so it was hanging over his face. He was wearing a surfing T-shirt and torn-up jeans.

I didn't know what to say. I couldn't tell if he really wanted to talk to us, or if he was just trying to recover from looking clumsy. Naturally, Patti didn't say a thing.

"What's up?" the boy asked, flipping his hair out of his eyes.

"Not much." I shrugged. "We're waiting for our friends."

He nodded. "That's cool. You live around here?"

"Not exactly," I said. "We're from Riverhurst."

He stared at me for a minute, then something seemed to register in his brain. "That's a couple of hours from here, right? I think my cousins live near there." He got back on his skateboard and started doing a few moves.

"Really? What's their name?" I asked.

"The Carlins," he said.

I turned to Patti. She looked as shocked as I felt! "You're not related to Jenny Carlin, are you?" she asked him.

"Sure thing," he said, swiveling back and forth on his board.

I started to snicker. Jenny Carlin is one of the few people in our class who we don't get along with — at all! She's always doing something mean behind our backs. "Jenny Carlin, huh?" I murmured. I couldn't believe it. Here I was, thinking maybe this guy wasn't too bad.

"Do you know her?" he asked, flipping his hair back again.

"Yeah, we're in the same class," I said. Watching him fix his hair every twenty seconds made me believe they actually *were* related. Jenny is pretty conceited about her looks, too.

"Cool," he said. "She's not like my first cousin. I think she's like my eighth once removed or something like that." He shrugged. "I've only seen her once. She was kind of a drag, actually." He twirled around on his board.

"Yeah, she can be," I said, winking at Patti, who looked as if she was going to burst out laughing any second. "So, what's your name? I mean, so I can tell Jenny I saw you," I said.

82

"Brian," he said. "Who are you?"

"I'm Lauren, and this is Patti," I said.

"Living way out in Riverhurst must be a real bummer," Brian commented as he tried to jump over the top three steps.

"It's okay." I frowned. "There are lots of good things about it."

"Like what?" he asked.

"Like you don't have to take the bus everywhere," I said. "And there are lots of trees."

"We have trees here," said Brian. "You just have to go to the park."

Suddenly Patti jumped up. "The park! That's it!" she cried.

"Well, it's, like, an okay park. It's nothing to get that excited about." Brian looked at Patti as if she were crazy.

"Don't you get it, Lauren? The park!" she said again.

I was beginning to wonder if the sun was getting to her. "What about it?" I asked.

"Don't you remember — Chris Mitchell has a baseball game at the park this afternoon!"

"That's right!" I said, standing up. "How far is it from here?" I asked Brian.

"About two blocks that way," he said. "Why?"

"There's someone we have to meet up with," I said. "See you later!"

"I can't believe we didn't think of this before," said Patti as we hurried along the sidewalk. "He can give us enough money to get some food, and then we can all go to the train station together."

"*If* he's still there." I pointed to my watch. "It's almost three o'clock."

"Hey, wait up!"

I turned around and saw Brian scooting after us on his skateboard.

"I think he likes you," Patti said, glancing over her shoulder at Brian.

"Get real!" I said.

"Well, he's not following *me*," Patti said as Brian came up beside us.

"I'll walk you to the park," he said, smiling at me. "Hey, you want to try my board?"

"No, thanks," I said. The sidewalks had too many cracks and bumps, and I didn't want to make a total fool out of myself by falling on my face.

"Then you can pull me, okay?" Brian took my elbow, and I dragged him along the sidewalk for a few feet.

"Come on, we'd better run!" said Patti. "We don't want to miss him." She took off, and I tried to

run after her. Have you ever tried to run while someone is holding onto your elbow? It's not very easy,
believe me.

"Whoa!" All of a sudden, Brian wasn't holding
on anymore. With a big crash, he fell to the ground.

"Sorry," I said, turning around and stopping for
a second.

"That's okay, I didn't need this leg anyway," he
said. Then he smiled. I couldn't help noticing he did
have a really nice smile!

Chapter 9

Patti and I were only a block away from the park when a group of boys in baseball uniforms passed us. "I hope we're not too late!" she said.

"The way this day is going, we probably are," I said. Then I turned and looked at Brian, who was still trying to hop the curb on his skateboard. Okay, so the day hadn't been *all* bad. We ran into the park.

"Look," Patti cried.

I stopped for a second and looked around. The park was huge! There were about twenty games going on at the same time. I had never seen a park so big — it was a hundred times the size of the one in River- hurst. I guess that only makes sense, though, since there are a hundred times more people in the city.

"We'll have to make a big circle and check out each game," said Patti.

"I'll wait over there," said Brian. He headed over to a playground that had been converted into a skateboard area — there were all kinds of ramps and loops, and kids flying every which way on them.

"Okay," I said, and we started our search. The first few games were being played by adults, so that was easy. But the next few were made up of kids Chris's age, and it was really hard to tell if he was playing because everyone had on caps! We had no idea what team we were looking for. At least a lot of games were still going on, so that was a good sign.

The park was filled with all kinds of people doing different things. Some people were lying out on blankets in their bathing suits, some were playing volleyball or Frisbee, and there were a lot of joggers and people on rollerblades going around the big loop on the edge of the park. The roller blades looked fun.

"Stop daydreaming, Lauren!" I looked up and saw Patti waving to me from the next baseball diamond. "Come on!" she yelled.

We must have run the whole way around that park. When we stopped at one of the only diamonds we hadn't checked yet, I leaned over and rubbed my foot. My blister was back in full force, and I felt like taking off my shoes and going barefoot. The problem was, you couldn't do that in the city — not even in the park. "Maybe we should go back to the travel agency," I said to Patti as we scanned the field. "Maybe Becky has some more candy bars in her desk."

Patti shook her head. "We'll find him," she said. "Just give me a few more minutes." She stared out at the players on the field. Would it be totally uncool to ask Brian to buy us a pizza? I wondered. He might think I was trying to ask him out. But, he might not. Either way, we might at least end up with lunch. I was about to suggest it to Patti when there was a loud *smack!* The batter had hit the ball deep into left field. I love watching baseball. The fielder sprinted back to catch the ball, only he went too far back, so then he had to run forward. His cap fell off as he dove for the ball. I wasn't sure if he caught it or not. Then he stood up, holding his glove in the air so everyone could see he had it.

"All right!" Patti yelled, grabbing my arm and jumping up and down.

I looked at her out of the corner of my eye. It was a good play, but it wasn't *that* good.

"Way to go, Chris!" she screamed, loud enough for the entire city to hear.

"Chris?" I murmured. "*The* Chris?" I stared out at left field. It was really him! I shook off Patti's hand and ran out onto the field.

"Hey, what are you doing?" The pitcher glared at me.

"We're trying to *play* here, in case you haven't noticed," the first baseman added.

I felt my face turning bright pink. "Right. Sorry," I said, walking backward off the field.

"I guess we'll have to wait until the next out," said Patti with a big grin. "Aren't you glad he's here?"

I nodded. "I just wish I hadn't made an idiot of myself."

Patti shrugged. "It's okay, I'm used to it." She laughed. "Anyway, you'll never see these people again. Don't worry."

The pitcher struck out the next batter so the side was retired. Chris had obviously seen us — how could he miss us, after what I had done? — and he ran over. "Hi!" he said. "I didn't think you would make it. We started late because of the thunderstorm."

"Well, we almost didn't make it," said Patti.

"Wait, where are your friends?" he asked.

"It's a long story," I said. "The gist of it is that we lost them, and we don't have any money."

"You're kidding!" Chris looked at Patti. "Are you okay? Are they okay? What happened?"

"We're fine," she said. "But we were wondering if, well, you could maybe get us something to eat. Then we're going to meet Kate and Stephanie at the train at 4:14."

Chris nodded. "Sure, we can do that. We only have one more inning to go, okay? Then we'll grab some food."

"Mitchell, you're up!" the coach yelled.

Chris ran over to his bench, grabbed a bat, and stepped up to the plate. I know it wasn't very nice of me, but I kept trying to send vibes to the pitcher: *Strike him out, strike him out.* I wanted the inning to be over as soon as possible!

I guess the pitcher didn't hear me. Chris hit a double, and the next guy hit a single. I sat down on the grass and sighed. I love baseball, but it is the slowest game in the universe!

✦ ✦ ✦ ✦ ✦ ✦

"Stephanie, you already have six things to try on. You can't take any more!" I said. The truth was,

I couldn't take any more — any more shopping, that is.

"Well, okay. I guess I'll go to the dressing room," she replied.

"I'll wait here," I said. I sat down on a bench outside the dressing room in Leland's junior department and took my notebook out of my knapsack. It was going to be a long wait, so I thought I might as well do something.

I considered writing an article for *It's Elementary,* the newspaper that our classroom, 5B, publishes. "How to Enjoy Your Trip to the City," I wrote at the top of the page.

Number one: Make sure you and your friends stick together.

Two: Make sure everyone has enough money in case of emergency.

Three: Make a list of what you're going to do and stick to it.

"Kate, do you like this?" Stephanie walked out of the dressing room wearing a red tank top with black around the neckline and the hem. She rarely wears anything that's not red, black, or white, or a combination of these three.

"It's great," I said. "Why don't you get it? Then we can get out of here."

"Not yet!" Stephanie acted as if I had suggested we jump off a cliff. She went back into the dressing room. I went back to my article.

Four: Don't let a friend railroad you into doing something you don't feel like doing.

I tapped the pencil against the rim of my hat while I tried to think of other hints to add to the list. I had bought a black felt hat that had a black ribbon band. Stephanie really liked it, and she said she would buy it from me after we got home. I didn't think I'd ever wear it again, but it was working well — no one had noticed me since I'd put it on. It was something to keep in mind in case I ever got another bad haircut.

I decided to skip the article and do something more important: plot the movie I wanted to make for my next Video Club project. Stephanie came out a few more times to show me her outfits. She was leaning toward buying a red-and-black-checked cotton jacket. I told her it looked fantastic on her. It did, with her long, black curly hair. Anything! Buy anything so we can leave! I thought. I wasn't seeing much of the city from the inside of Leland's Department Store.

Stephanie stared at herself in the mirror for a minute. Then she grabbed the hat from my head.

"Hey!" I cried. "Give that back."

"I just want to see how it looks with the jacket," she said. "It'll only take a second. After all, I *am* buying this from you."

"Oh, all right." I scrunched down on the bench and held my notebook up in front of my face.

"I swear, Kate, you are getting so paranoid." Stephanie turned a few times in front of the three-way-mirror. "Okay, I'll buy it. We can go now."

"Hurray!" I jumped up and stuffed the notebook back in my knapsack, then walked up to the cash register with Stephanie.

"Look, Mom, it's that girl who's on the cover of *Theater Times*," a girl behind us in line whispered. "Excuse me, but aren't you — "

"Sarah Spinney?" I said. "No, I'm not." I took the hat off Stephanie's head and pulled it down over my ears. "I'm nobody, okay?"

"It's true," Stephanie told the girl. "She really is nobody."

"Thanks a lot!" I said.

"Hey, you said it first," she said.

Before we could get into another argument, the sales clerk rang up the jacket. Stephanie paid for it, and finally, we were ready to leave.

"What time is it?" Stephanie asked. "Maybe we still have time for one more store." Once Patti, Lauren, and I bought her a bumper sticker that said, So MUCH SHOPPING, So LITTLE TIME! Until she has a car to put it on, she's keeping it on her bulletin board.

"No, I don't think so," I said. "It's three-thirty."

Stephanie's face lit up. "Good, we have loads of time! We can check out that shoe store I was telling you about. It's right down here somewhere." She looked around at the different stores. "Maybe they moved."

"What a shame," I said. "I think we should start heading for the train station. We definitely don't want to get there late."

"But it's only about a five-minute walk from here," Stephanie argued. "We don't have to go yet. I have an idea — let's buy something for Lauren and Patti."

That's one of the best things about Stephanie: She's very generous. She doesn't mind spending her shopping energy — or her money — on her friends.

"See that store? I bet we can get something nice there," she said.

"Well, okay," I agreed. "But we can only stay for fifteen minutes."

Stephanie laughed. "You sound like my mother!"

It was really cool inside — they sold all kinds of cards and postcards, posters, gag gifts, and T-shirts. I knew we could find something for Lauren and Patti, and for us too!

"Let's get this for Lauren!" Stephanie held up a miniature pink refrigerator. I looked inside. It even had miniature ice-cube trays and a miniature carton of milk.

"It's perfect," I said. "What should we get Patti?"

We looked around the store for a few minutes. Then I heard Stephanie cry, "Kate, over here!" She was pointing at a T-shirt hanging on the wall that said SAVE THE PLANET on the front, and NOW! on the back. Both Patti and Stephanie are really involved in projects to clean up the environment.

"She'll love it," I said.

"I think we might have to get something for us, too," said Stephanie. She handed me a mug that said

I'M THE BOSS! on it. "This is for you."

"No, I think it's for *you*," I said, smiling.

"I know, let's get two," she said. "That way we can both be the boss."

We took our gifts up to the counter and paid for them. As we walked out of the store, I took a quick peek at my watch and let out a gasp. "Oh, no! It's almost four o'clock!"

Chapter 10

We ran into the train station so fast that my hat went flying off my head. Stephanie was right behind me and she stopped to pick it up, even though her hands were full of bags. "Here, Sarah," she said.

I jammed it back on my head, and we hurried over to the board that listed all the departing trains. "That's ours! The 4:14 to Ridgemont. It says it's on time." I checked my watch. "That means it's going to leave in ten minutes!"

Stephanie set down the shopping bags and stood on her tiptoes to look around the station. "I don't see them anywhere."

"That's what we've been saying all day." I bit my lip. "I hope they're okay."

"I'll go check the track and see if they're waiting

down there," Stephanie offered. "Watch the bags."
As I stood and waited for Stephanie to come back, I
took off the floppy hat and put it in one of the bags.
I wanted to be sure Patti and Lauren would recognize
me — and it was well worth the risk of being mistaken for Sarah Spinney! I stared at everyone who
walked by, hoping it would be them. I heard a loud
click and looked up: The clock on the departure
board had just changed to 4:05.

Stephanie came back, panting because she was
out of breath. "They're not down there."

"I can't believe this," I said. "Why aren't they
here?"

"There's still plenty of time. They'll make it,"
Stephanie assured me.

"Maybe we should have them paged," I told
Stephanie.

"That's a good idea. Do you want to go, or
should I?"

"You go, and I'll stay here," I said. The clock
ticked to 4:06. I got up on one of the benches so I
could look around the station. Stephanie was making
her way through the crowd to the customer service
desk. There was a line about ten people long. By the
time we paged Lauren and Patti, the train would be
long gone!

It was 4:10 when Stephanie came back. "Maybe we should get on the train," she said. "Maybe they're already home! We could call the Mitchells and find out."

I shook my head. "We're not leaving here without them."

A policewoman tapped me on the leg. "Young lady, no standing on the chairs," she said. "Please get down."

"I can't — it's an emergency," I told her.

"I'm sorry, rules are rules. You could get hurt. Now, get down." She looked serious, so I stepped down onto the floor. "What's the emergency?"

Just then the public address system crackled, and a woman said, "Will the party traveling with Kate Beekman and Stephanie Green please meet them under the departure board immediately."

"That's us," I told the policewoman.

"Fine. Now you don't need to be standing on any chairs," she said.

"This will be the final boarding call for train 525, departing at 4:14 for Ridgemont," the announcer's voice crackled over the public address system. "All passengers should proceed directly to track 17. I repeat, this is the final boarding call."

"We'd better run!" a familiar voice called out.

99

"My parents will kill me if I don't make this train!"

Suddenly, Stephanie looked as if she were going to explode. "Can you believe it?" she said.

"What?" I said.

She pointed straight ahead of her to a bunch of guys in baseball uniforms. One of them was Chris — and right behind him were Patti and Lauren, running at top speed toward track 17!

"Lauren!" I cried, jumping up and down. "Over here!"

She stopped and looked around, confused.

"I just can't believe it," Stephanie repeated. "Here we were, going crazy, practically losing our minds *worrying* about Lauren and Patti, and it turns out they've been spending the whole afternoon hanging out with Chris and his friends!"

"Lauren! Patti!" I yelled again. Stephanie and I grabbed our shopping bags and bolted after them. "Lauren, it's us!" I cried.

She turned around. I had never seen such a big smile on her face as I did then — except if you count the time she discovered s'mores back in kindergarten. "Kate!" she screamed.

I ran up to her and threw my arms around her. "I'm so glad you're all right! I'm so sorry!"

"It's not your fault," she said.

100

"Yeah, well, it *is* going to be your fault if we miss this train," said Chris, tugging at our sleeves. "Come on!"

Stephanie stopped hugging Patti, and we all ran down the stairs. The doors on the train were already closing, but Chris held them open until we all got on.

"Where were you when we needed you?" Lauren joked.

We walked through the train until we found a bunch of seats together.

"So?" I said as soon as we were settled. "What happened to you?"

"It doesn't look as if you had too bad a day," Stephanie commented in a low voice, looking over at Chris and his buddies.

"It was *horrible*," said Lauren. "First we had this really grouchy bus driver. Then we walked the thirty blocks back to the museum — and you guys were gone!"

"We were only gone for a little while," I said. "We left you a note, but I guess you didn't get it."

"I think we might have," said Patti. "Only we couldn't read it because it got all wet in the storm."

"I told you I saw Patti over there," I said to Stephanie.

"Where were you?" asked Lauren.

"In the coffee shop across the street," Stephanie answered.

Lauren looked at Patti and said, "*Well! Some* of us ate well today."

"Sorry. Did you get anything to eat?" I asked.

"Yeah, we had some candy bars around two-thirty," said Patti. "Then we met this cute guy who asked for Lauren's address. . . ."

"What?" Stephanie cried.

"Yeah, he's pretty nice, too," said Lauren. "His name is Brian. The only problem is, he's Jenny Carlin's cousin!"

"You're *kidding!*" I said. "So how can he be cute and nice?"

Lauren shrugged. "It's a mystery, I know."

"So then what happened?" I asked.

"Patti remembered that Chris had a game in the park. It wasn't that far from the museum, so we went over and met up with him. After the game, he bought us a couple of hot dogs." Lauren rubbed her stomach. "I don't know if that was such a hot idea after the candy bar. I feel like the president of the National Junk Food Association."

I burst out laughing. It was so great to have

Lauren back. Even though it had been just one day, it seemed like forever!

"Okay, now let me get this straight." Stephanie drummed her fingernails on the arm of her seat. "Kate and I sat around on the museum steps all day waiting for you. We thought you were completely miserable. We were afraid we'd never see you again." She paused and then spoke in a lower voice. "We didn't do anything fun. And it turns out that you were meeting some hunk, and then you got to hang out with Chris!" She folded her arms across her chest and stared out the window. "Life is not fair," she said.

"Steph, don't take this the wrong way, but you didn't exactly spend the whole day suffering," I said. I pointed to the five shopping bags under her seat.

She didn't say anything.

"What did you guys do?" Patti asked.

"We looked all over for you, first of all. Then we waited on the steps. We went to lunch — and talked to some cute guys. Then we went back to the steps. Finally, around three o'clock, we went shopping. It was inevitable," I said, pointing at Stephanie.

"What did you get?" asked Patti.

I knew that would perk Stephanie right up, and it did. She pulled everything out of the bags to show them her new sandals for summer, her new light-weight jacket, and her new shades. "Oh, this is Kate's," she said, handing me the hat.

Lauren giggled. "Are you going for a new image, or what?"

"It just so happens that I needed a disguise today," I said. "Stephanie, tell them how we got separated in the first place."

Patti leaned forward. "Yes, I was wondering what happened."

"Well, we were right behind you," Stephanie began. "And all of a sudden, this girl comes up and wants Kate's autograph."

"Why?" said Lauren.

"Because she thought Kate was this actress named Sarah Spinney. And that was only the beginning," said Stephanie. "People kept coming up to her all day. Have you ever heard of Sarah Spinney?"

Patti and Lauren shook their heads.

"So, was it the worst birthday on record?" I asked Patti.

"No, not really," she said.

Stephanie looked over at Chris and then winked at her. "I'll bet!"

Patti just blushed. She hates it when we tease her about boys. She doesn't even like to talk about them that much, which is kind of funny because a lot of them seem to like her.

"Well, we'll make up for your birthday tonight," I promised Patti. "Did Lauren tell you we were going to take you out to lunch?"

"Yeah. That would have been fun. Maybe next time," said Patti.

"Oh, I don't know if we should go to that restaurant where all the celebrities hang out," Lauren said in a serious voice. "People might start hounding Kate for her autograph." She cracked up laughing.

As the train pulled into the station, I saw the Mitchells *and* the Jenkinses standing on the platform, waiting for us. Horace was there, too, and he looked very worried. "Uh-oh," I said to Stephanie. "Remember that message we left on the machine?"

"You guys left a message, too?" asked Patti as we maneuvered down the aisle to the door.

"They're probably freaking out," said Lauren. "I told them we didn't have any money!"

"Prepare yourselves for a lecture," Stephanie said over her shoulder as she stepped off the train. One of Chris's better-looking friends helped her with all her bags, so I knew she wouldn't write off the day as a total loss.

The Jenkinses rushed over and threw their arms around all of us. It was kind of embarrassing, but to tell you the truth, I was pretty happy to see them, too!

We were all walking toward the van, explaining what had happened and why we'd left those frantic messages, when a woman ran over to us with an excited look on her face. I automatically reached for the hat, but it was too late.

"Sarah Spinney, what are you doing way out here?" she said, smiling from ear to ear. "You should have told the local paper you were coming. We would have organized a welcoming committee!"

Patti, Lauren, Stephanie, and Chris burst out laughing — and so did I.

Chapter 11

Once we got back to the Mitchells' house, we spent an hour explaining how we got separated and why we never met up again. It was amazing! We had missed Lauren and Patti so many times, and each time by only five minutes or so. We decided that we would always carry our own money from then on, and that we'd always have a Plan B. That way, if we ever did mess up the original plan, we'd have something to fall back on, and we wouldn't have to tromp all over town looking for each other.

Mr. and Mrs. Jenkins weren't mad at us. They just told us to be a lot more careful in the future. They said we had done the right thing by calling them, and by arranging way ahead of time to take the 4:14 train. They also said they trusted us, because we were mature enough to handle the situation. I couldn't remember being called "mature" before. The Jenkinses are pretty cool parents.

Mr. Mitchell convinced Patti to go in the backyard and help him set up the croquet set for later, so that the rest of us could decorate the dining room for Patti's special birthday dinner. We put up streamers and different-colored balloons all over. Mrs. Mitchell had ordered a big sheet cake from the bakery. It said HAPPY BIRTHDAY, PATTI! on it, natch, and the three of us got to add whatever we wanted to the decorations. I tried to draw a picture of Patti smiling, but it came out goofy. Lauren wrote HOORAY FOR PATTI!, and Stephanie, who's a really good artist, drew a cat that looked just like Patti's cat, Adelaide.

"Surprise!" we all yelled when Patti walked into the dining room later that evening.

She turned bright red and smiled. "Thanks!" She slid into her seat at the head of the table.

"Tell me the truth, were you surprised?" I asked, sitting down beside her.

"Sure," she said. "Not very, but a little," she whispered. "I didn't know there were going to be balloons."

The Mitchells and the Jenkinses had gone all out

for the meal. There was so much food on the table, like fried chicken and corn on the cob — Patti's favorites. (And mine, too.)

"Pass the salad, please, Sarah," Stephanie said to me.

"Ha-ha," I said.

"Who's Sarah?" asked Mrs. Mitchell.

"Remember how I told you that people kept confusing me with this celebrity? Well, I guess she's in some hit musical in town. I've never heard of her, though," I said. "So she can't be that big."

"Kate, you don't exactly keep up with the theater scene," Lauren observed.

"Yeah, only the movie theater scene," Patti added.

"So who is this person the whole city has you confused with?" Mr. Jenkins asked.

I waved my fork in the air. "Someone named Sarah Spinney."

"Sarah Spinney! I should have known! Excuse me, I'll be right back," said Mrs. Mitchell. She left the table and went into the kitchen. She came back a minute later carrying a newspaper. "This was in the recycling pile — I'm glad we still have it." She handed me the paper.

"What am I supposed to look at?" I asked.

"Right there!" Mrs. Mitchell pointed to an article with a headline: NEW ACTRESS SCORES A HIT WITH "BUGABOO." *Bugaboo?* Beneath the headline was a photo of a girl who looked about six years old.

"Tell me that's not her," I said, looking more closely at the picture.

"Let me see!" Stephanie demanded.

"Wait a second." I skimmed the article. Sarah Spinney was only eight years old! And what was worse, she looked even younger than that! "I do *not* look like this person," I said. Maybe my little sister, Melissa, did. But me? No way!

"Show us!" said Lauren.

I sighed and handed the paper down the table. "I think everyone in this city needs glasses," I said. "Maybe there's a shortage of eye doctors."

Stephanie and Lauren started giggling the second they saw the picture.

"I don't look like her, do I?" I asked.

"Well, we don't think so." Stephanie said putting the paper aside. "But if the rest of the city thinks so, and they saw the play . . ."

I glared at her and went back to eating my fried chicken.

* * *

After dinner, Mrs. Mitchell brought out the cake, and everyone sang "Happy Birthday" — even Chris, although his voice kept cracking.

"This is great!" Patti said, looking at all the different things we had drawn on the cake. Chris had added some miniature chocolate baseball bats. I held the plates, and Patti served the pieces onto them.

After we passed them out, Mrs. Jenkins carried in a big pile of presents and put them down next to Patti. "Open your presents!" Stephanie said.

I could tell Patti was embarrassed about being the center of attention, but she picked up the present on top of the stack. It was a gold necklace from her parents. They also gave her a subscription to a science magazine.

Stephanie had painted a big birthday card for Patti that was beautiful.

Lauren gave Patti a stuffed blue whale. Patti has a big collection of stuffed animals. "I know you're getting too old for these," said Lauren, "but this one was so cute! And the proceeds from the sales go toward preventing cruelty to animals."

"Thanks, I love it!" Patti said, squeezing the whale. She opened my present next. I'd edited all the film I'd taken of Patti over the past year and put it together onto one tape. "Wow, I can't believe you did all this!" Patti exclaimed. "Look, everyone, it's a movie!"

"What's it called?" asked Chris.

"*Patti: Part I,*" she said.

I shrugged. "It's not very original, but — "

"Let's watch it!" Chris called from the other end of the table.

I kicked Patti under the table. There were things on that tape no one but the Sleepover Friends should see!

"Uh, I think we'll watch it later," Patti said. "I still have some more presents to open." She picked up the next one. "This is weird. This one says it's for Lauren." She looked at Lauren. "Is it from you?"

"No, it's *for* her," I said. "It goes with that other one for you. They're not birthday presents, exactly."

"They're sorry-you-missed-out-on-all-the-fun-today presents," said Stephanie. "Not that I think you did," she added under her breath.

Lauren opened her package and pulled out the mini fridge. "It's just what I need!" she said, laughing. "Now I won't have to ask my parents for one."

"This shirt is really nice!" said Patti, holding up the T-shirt for everyone to see. "I'm going to wear it tomorrow. Thanks, you guys!" Patti got up from the table. "This has been a really great birthday."

"Wait — there's one more present." Chris ran into the living room and took something out from behind the TV. He walked over and handed it awkwardly to Patti. "Happy birthday."

I glanced at Stephanie. She was smiling, and I was glad she wasn't mad anymore about Chris liking Patti. He was so sweet! He had obviously liked Patti for a while, only she hadn't noticed because she's so modest.

Patti shyly unwrapped the package. It was pretty big, and I couldn't imagine what it was. She slowly pulled out a baseball glove — only instead of being new, it was all beat-up and worn in.

"It's my old glove," said Chris, "from when we used to play together. You said you didn't play much anymore, so I thought you needed some inspiration." He cleared his throat. "Plus, your parents told me you lost yours."

"Thanks," Patti said softly. She slipped the glove onto her hand and pounded it a few times with her fist. "It fits perfectly!"

Chris showed her what all the marks on it were from — like the tooth marks from when a dog had tried to run away with it. Then he and Patti went outside to play catch and try it out.

113

"Boys are so romantic," Stephanie commented wryly as we cleared the table.

"I think that was really nice," said Lauren. "They make a cute couple, don't you think? Kate?"

I was too busy staring at that Sarah Spinney picture to respond. Maybe it was time for me to change my looks. The next time I visited the city, I was not going to be mistaken for an eight-year-old!

✦ ✦ ✦ ✦ ✦ ✦

I know Kate's going to try to get the last word here, so I'm going to sneak in and tell you the rest of what happened that night before she gets a chance.

After we played croquet and had second helpings of birthday cake, it was ten o'clock. Chris and everyone else went upstairs to bed, leaving the living room to us.

Kate and I unfolded one of the couches and flopped down on it, while Stephanie and Patti unfolded the other one. "I can't believe everything that happened today!" I said.

"Neither can I," said Stephanie. "I thought we were going to be sitting on those museum steps forever."

"So did we," said Patti. "But you know what? It was a lot of fun."

"Come on, Patti — remember when we were

still sitting in that travel agency, soaking wet, and being lectured by Mr. Harmon?" I said. "That was not fun."

"You're right, it wasn't," she said. "There are a lot of weird people in the city, but there are a lot of nice people, too. Like Brian!" She grinned at me.

"Are you going to write to him?" asked Kate.

I wasn't sure about that. I'd only spent a little time with him. I liked him, but I wasn't sure if I really knew him. "I think I'll see if he writes me first," I said.

"This is going to be one of those stories where they start out as pen pals and then get married," said Stephanie.

Patti started laughing. "And — and — then you'll be related to Jenny Carlin!"

I threw a pillow at her. "Never! Anyway, *you're* the one with the big romance."

"Shhh!" She pointed at the ceiling. "He might hear us."

"Patti, I just have one question: Who are you going to choose, Henry or Chris?" asked Stephanie. "Truth or dare?"

Patti shook her head. "I didn't say I was playing Truth or Dare."

"Oh, come on," Stephanie said.

"I don't have to choose either one," Patti said.

"Oh! So you have two boyfriends now!" Kate teased her.

"No, I don't!" Patti protested. Her face was beet-red. "Cut it out!"

"Okay, we'll leave you alone," Stephanie said. "But what are you going to tell Henry when he asks you about that glove?"

Patti shrugged. "I'll tell him an old friend gave it to me."

"Mm-hm." Stephanie nodded. "And you think he'll believe that?"

Patti got up and walked over to my bed. "You know what, Lauren? I'm beginning to wish we'd never found them."

"Oh, yeah?" Kate yelled. "Well, take that!" she said, hurling a pillow at us.

"And this is for making us worry about you!" Stephanie flung a pillow at my ear.

"Girls, is everything all right down there?" Mrs. Jenkins called from the stairs. "I hope you're getting ready for bed — we have a long drive tomorrow!"

"We are, Mom!" Patti answered.

"Okay, then, good-night," said Mrs. Jenkins. "Sleep tight!"

"We will!" Patti said.

116

When we heard Mrs. Jenkins close her bedroom door upstairs, we all cracked up laughing.

"So, who wants another piece of cake?" I asked.

Kate scooted up to the TV. "I'll see what movies are on."

"Patti, come over here, I want to try something with your hair," said Stephanie.

Sleepover Friends forever!

SLEEPOVER FRIENDS™

by Susan Saunders

Available wherever you buy books...or use this order form.

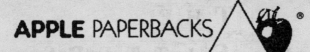
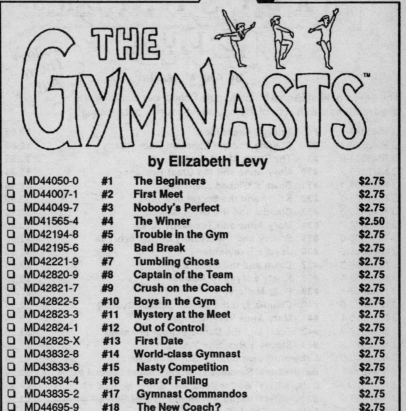

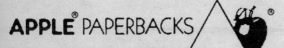

APPLE® PAPERBACKS

Pick an Apple and Polish Off Some Great Reading!

BEST-SELLING APPLE TITLES

❑ MT42975-2	The Bullies and Me Harriet Savitz	$2.75
❑ MT42709-1	Christina's Ghost Betty Ren Wright	$2.75
❑ MT41682-0	Dear Dad, Love Laurie Susan Beth Pfeffer	$2.75
❑ MT43461-6	The Dollhouse Murders Betty Ren Wright	$2.75
❑ MT42545-5	Four Month Friend Susan Clymer	$2.75
❑ MT43444-6	Ghosts Beneath Our Feet Betty Ren Wright	$2.75
❑ MT44351-8	Help! I'm a Prisoner in the Library Eth Clifford	$2.75
❑ MT43188-9	The Latchkey Kids Carol Anshaw	$2.75
❑ MT44567-7	Leah's Song Eth Clifford	$2.75
❑ MT43618-X	Me and Katie (The Pest) Ann M. Martin	$2.75
❑ MT41529-8	My Sister, The Creep Candice F. Ransom	$2.75
❑ MT42883-7	Sixth Grade Can Really Kill You Barthe DeClements	$2.75
❑ MT40409-1	Sixth Grade Secrets Louis Sachar	$2.75
❑ MT42882-9	Sixth Grade Sleepover Eve Bunting	$2.75
❑ MT41732-0	Too Many Murphys Colleen O'Shaughnessy McKenna	$2.75
❑ MT42326-6	Veronica the Show-Off Nancy K. Robinson	$2.75

Available wherever you buy books, or use this order form.

- -

Scholastic Inc., P.O. Box 7502, 2931 East McCarty Street, Jefferson City, MO 65102

Please send me the books I have checked above. I am enclosing $_____ (please add $2.00 to cover shipping and handling). Send check or money order — no cash or C.O.D.s please.

Name _____

Address _____

City_____ State/Zip _____

Please allow four to six weeks for delivery. Offer good in the U.S.A. only. Sorry, mail orders are not available to residents of Canada. Prices subject to change.

APP1090